BROKEN SAMURAI

BROKEN SAMURAI

One Marine's Journey from Hero to Hitman

Development of the Violent Mind
Book 3

AL CARLISLE, PHD

Broken Samurai:
One Marine's Journey
from Hero to Hitman

Al Carlisle, PhD

Book Three in the *Development*
***of the Violent Mind* Series**

The stories and recollections in this book are taken from interviews and correspondence with "Danny." The accuracy of these events may be marred with historic discrepancies due to the passage of time and the cognitive nature of PTSD.

ISBN: 978-1-952043-06-2

Library of Congress Control Number: 2020931146

Third Edition: January 2020 by Carlisle Legacy Books, LLC

Second edition: 2017 by Genius Book Publishing

First edition: 2016 by Genius Book Publishing

First edition edited by Dr. Michael R. Collings

Second edition revised by Leya Booth

Third edition revised by Charlene Harmon, Carrie Anne Keller, Dave Taylor, and Steve Harmon

Cover art designed by C. Lindsay Carlisle with art by pixabay.com

Published by Carlisle Legacy Books, LLC
https://www.carlislelegacybooks.com

❀ Created with Vellum

Contents

Preface: The Boy - Part 1

In the mid-1980s, a ten-year-old boy was walking home after a long evening with friends. It was 2:00 am, and his mother was undoubtedly worried. The boy took a shortcut down an alley, where he skirted garbage cans and trash stacked behind a row of apartments. As he reached the end of the alley and turned onto the street, a shiny black Chrysler passed him and parked less than a block ahead.

As the driver stopped the car and got out, a scruffy-looking man walked towards him. The boy stepped behind a tree so he wouldn't be seen.

He heard a man asking for a light for his cigarette. He peered around the tree to watch and, as the driver reached into his jacket for a lighter, the scruffy man pulled out a pistol. The boy heard two shots, and the driver fell to the ground, dead.

The boy was terrified. He ran back down the alley, away from what he had just witnessed. About halfway down the alley, he ducked behind a large trash can. If the killer had seen him, he might think the boy had made it to the other end of the alley or perhaps had gone in the back door of one of the apartments.

As he crouched against the wall, he heard somebody coming down the alley. He held still, praying the killer wouldn't find him.

He heard garbage cans being shifted. The killer was searching for him.

The trash can he was hiding behind jerked away, exposing him. As he looked up at the killer, he cried, "Please, mister, don't kill me."

Two quick shots ended the boy's life.

Several years later, I became acquainted with that killer. His name was Danny. He was a hit man for a biker's club. I was surprised to learn that he was also a highly decorated Vietnam combat veteran. Since killing the boy, he had been haunted by what he referred to as the boy's ghost. In fact, he had been, and was still being, haunted by the ghosts of the many people he had killed, in both Vietnam and since coming home.

Danny willingly participated in my study on killers. He wanted people to more fully understand the impact combat can have on the mind of a teenager unprepared for war. Danny had been a relatively normal boy from a normal family when he volunteered to serve his country in the war in Vietnam, hoping to stop communism from taking over the world. His experiences in Vietnam (and those of other combat veterans I have worked with) had a profound effect on him, more so than the vast majority of PTSD (Post-Traumatic Stress Disorder) clients I have seen who had not experienced the trauma of war. Like so many others, Danny returned home vastly changed. He may have left Vietnam, but Vietnam never left Danny.

This book is not like other books about PTSD you may

read. It is not a story of a single event, and it is not simply a story of Danny's tour in Vietnam. This book is specifically about PTSD stemming from combat, and war PTSD differs markedly from other kinds of PTSD. It should be given its own designation, with separate treatments to fit its unique problems.

All wars provide the basis for PTSD, but the experience of each veteran is different from the next. Some have had horrendous, traumatic experiences, while others were spared the blood, the gore, and the guilt. Some soldiers shrank in fear when the mortars began exploding around them. Others became angry and aggressive, and fought in hopes of getting revenge. Some came home with a deep sigh of relief at having returned alive. Others wished to return to the war, even though they believed there was a good chance that this time they might not come home alive.

I have come to believe that no matter how much training a person has, he cannot witness death in war—whether of his own people or of the enemy—and not suffer dramatic changes to his personality. Some vets won't talk about their trauma, burying it deep in their mind. Others feel driven to find peace by seeking answers. Some combat soldiers cling tightly to their religious beliefs, while others lose theirs. Danny had lost his belief in God when he was quite young, and substituted a belief in ancient traditions that was as strong for him as a dedication to God is for others. He modeled his life on the Samurai.

Danny died from a stroke at the age of 48. This is his story.

Since this book first was published, some people have had a difficult time reading it. Some have felt sorry for Danny. Veterans have said it stirred up too many memories of their own combat trauma. Some said they wanted to see some indication of hope for Danny, and for others who have fought for our country. In this second edition, I have attempted to offer hope rather than condemnation.

As a psychologist, before talking to veterans I was unaware of the extent of the overpowering effects of war them. Most vets do not talk about these things and they aren't detailed in mental health textbooks. Mental health professionals need a more complete understanding of war, even if we hear or read things that frighten us. I have reported what Danny said in his own words and I have made no attempt to dramatize it. What he said was from his heart.

ONE

Khe Sanh and the Tet Offensive

When I first began meeting with Danny he was apparently willing to talk about his past. He told me what it was like growing up in Illinois, why he joined the Marines, and about experiences he had during the war. He talked about what he went through when he came back to America, and why he got into a biker group. However, one day he came into my office and said,

> As much as we have covered and as much as I do understand already, there are certain things that we didn't go into in enough depth.
> I tried at the time to get things said but some things were really hard to say. You know? But once we got past that, maybe now it's time to dig into it a little deeper.

As a therapist and researcher, I'm the one who usually suggests that we go deeper into an issue or an event. But, in this case, it was Danny, and it was clear that Danny wanted to tell me something.

How do you mean? Got past what?

> I have never really understood why I changed so much in Vietnam. There were a lot of other combat Marines who changed as well, but not to the same degree that I did.

What do you mean when you say you got past something? What do you want to do now?

> I've given you a general overview of the situation but I'm not fully comfortable with it. I feel there is still something missing. At times when we got through with an interview I was all right with what I told you, but later that night I felt I had left something out.

Was it that there were things that happened in Vietnam that you weren't ready to talk about?

> Some, yeah. I did some things in Nam that I haven't told anyone. But it's more than that. When I first got into therapy, I was defensive and I thought I was right and everybody else was wrong. I had done things that were wrong in the eyes of society, but not

in my eyes. Kate [his therapist] helped me see that maybe I was wrong. I've talked about a lot of my experiences but I feel that there are connections that I'm still not making within myself. It's like I'm trying to put together a big puzzle and there are some pieces still missing.

This didn't appear to be a confession. It was more like he was beginning to see that he had been lying to himself and wanted to look more deeply within. I wondered, was he willing to accept responsibility for his actions? If so, why now?

Through our sessions, it had become clear that Danny was hiding from himself. When he initially got into counseling, his therapist emphasized the advantages of understanding himself as he actually was rather than the fantasized image of himself he had created. Perhaps he was ready to open up on a deeper level because he wanted to see what he was really like on the inside. We decided that we would begin with his initial experiences in Vietnam and go from there.

Where do you want to start?

It began for me at Khe Sanh.

You said earlier that there were about 6,000 Marines sent there. What happened?

In my group there were 1,100 Marines and support people. So that's about 1,000 rifles. There were other Marine units up there as well. There were about 6,000 Marines in all.

What were your expectations when you were sent up there?

We were to guard the airstrip. We were close to the Demilitarized Zone and Laos, and we were to try to stop military supplies from coming from the north along the Ho Chi Minh Trail into South Vietnam. That area of the country was very mountainous and we were in a valley surrounded by these mountains. Suddenly we were bombarded from these mountains by the North Vietnamese Army.

How bad was it?

The attack had already started when I got there. We were terrified. We had believed there was only a small number of the enemy up there, and suddenly there were enemy mortar rounds coming down on us from these hills. At first we didn't know where they were coming from. The mortar rounds kept dropping down on us, and we just tried to keep from getting killed.

When I first flew into the Khe Sanh base the landing strip looked like a junkyard, an aircraft junkyard. We had C-130 aircraft on the strip rolled off to the side. There were all these piled-up, burned-out helicopters;

everything that had been hit by the enemy. They had that airstrip zeroed in with mortars and artillery, and they blew our planes up. You see, we initially got supplied by those planes after they cut off the road. Right then, when they started to blow the planes up, our military started flying over with planes and dropping our stuff to us, our bullets and our food and stuff by parachute. And then the NVA would shoot at those planes. We had forward observers who tried to detect where these antiaircraft guns were firing from and we would fire back at their positions.

~

American armed forces in South Vietnam were fighting against the Vietcong. The North Vietnamese Army (NVA), with its headquarters in Hanoi, was a well-trained military force but hadn't yet fully entered into the war. Military intelligence had detected movement by the NVA in the northern section of South Vietnam, suggesting that Hanoi might be preparing for something but, as yet, just what was not clear.

Americans back home were ambivalent about the war. World War I was supposed to have been the war that ended all wars. But then came World War II, and then Korea, and now Vietnam. We had been constantly under the threat of a nuclear war with Russia. People had built underground bomb shelters and equipped them with food, guns, and ammunition in case we were attacked by the Soviets.

We didn't want to be involved in another war, but we didn't want communist regimes taking over the world. If South Vietnam, which wanted democracy, fell to the communist government of North Vietnam, communism could spread to Laos and Cambodia and who knew where from there. When we got involved, due to a commitment to the South Vietnam government, our government assured us that the loss of American lives would be minimal.

However, this war was not like previous wars. We were fighting guerrilla warfare with the Vietcong (Vietnamese communists). They were a ghost military, locals working in the rice fields or in the cities during the day and by night killing Americans and villagers who cooperated with Americans. They controlled villages through fear. The people in South Vietnam wanted democracy but, at the same time, they didn't want Americans in their country. It was a love-hate relationship.

When the war didn't end as quickly as we had been led to believe it would, and the number of American deaths increased, the American people, particularly college students, became nervous about the war. The government responded by sending over more troops.

Vietnam has a major holiday at the end of January, called Tet, a week-long celebration in which families get together and conduct religious ceremonies. Traditionally, if a war was going on, the factions would not fight during Tet. In 1968, half of the South Vietnamese military had been allowed to go back to their villages to be with their families.

Danny arrived in Vietnam that January, and a week later he and other Marines were flown to an area close to the Demilitarized Zone (DMZ) to guard the landing strip at Khe Sanh. They were unaware that for the past several months the NVA and the Vietcong had been planning a coordinated country-wide attack on villages and cities, believing that the citizens of South Vietnam would rise up against the Americans and the South Vietnam government and America would withdraw its troops.

The surprise attack became known as the Tet Offensive. It was a major turning point in the war. While the Viet Cong stormed the cities and villages in the south, the NVA began their attack in the north. It was a massive, well-coordinated attack, one from which South Vietnam, and America, would never recover.

Khe Sanh is a valley in the north. The military had an airbase there, a landing strip and a few supply buildings. The village of Khe Sanh, for which the airbase was named, lay a few miles away. It was empty; the villagers had been moved elsewhere several years before. Because the base was surrounded by mountains, the enemy could hide there and not be detected.

Danny was transported to Khe Sanh by chopper since the enemy had cut off vehicle access into their area by blowing up the bridges on National Route 9, which runs east and west from Dong Ha across Vietnam into Laos. Even transportation by aircraft was difficult because mortar rounds constantly bombarded the landing strip and the Marine positions there.

In Danny's case, escape to the south was cut off. It was extremely risky for any plane to attempt a landing there. Mortar rounds punched holes in the runway, which had to be continually patched up. Even aircraft flying over to drop supplies were targeted. Danny and the Marines with him were isolated, with no means of escape. It must have been terrifying.

. . .

Did you feel you might not live through it?

You know, that's funny, because I don't think that anybody felt they would be getting out.

Really?

I know it is a contradiction. We felt like we would hold, but one day we took over 1100 rounds of artillery, rockets and mortars, in six and a half hours. A Khe Sanh day was like that. They had dead straight shots into us from these hills. They had us stuck in one spot and we couldn't move and they knew it, so they zeroed in on us.

They could fire in and they could observe where the round hit and they could adjust for the next round. They could do whatever they wanted to. They pounded us ... on a regular basis. There was a little bit of harassment fire at night, but during the daytime they laid wood to us. They fired in on us all the time.

Okay. So here you are and you've got the enemy all around you.

Yeah, we later learned that there were between 20,000 and 40,000 of them that had surrounded us.

The enemy is out there. You can't see where they are. There is no retreat, there is no getting out of there. You know that reinforcements should be coming but incoming planes could be blown out of the sky with a direct hit. Did you think that reinforcements might not make it on time?

Well, there were some jokes made to that effect, but the people that were around me that I dealt with day

> in and day out felt that we could hold, you know. We
> didn't know until after Khe Sanh what their side,
> their strength was. We only knew that they were
> strong enough to cut off the road and the only way
> we could be supplied was by air.
> I would bet that most guys felt we were going to die
> there. But it was funny because nobody would allow
> you to give up.

That would be very depressing.

> It wasn't a depressing feeling. I know that sounds
> strange.

Yes, it does.

How does the mind survive under conditions in which death appears almost inevitable? Only weeks before, Danny had been home with his family, his friends, and his girlfriend. He had been taught that it was a sin to kill. He had joined the Marines expecting to go to Vietnam but anticipated a short war. His Marine training conditioned in him that it was not only all right to kill under certain conditions, but that it was the best way to stay alive. He was now surrounded by the enemy, and it appeared that they would likely not live through it. He saw the bodies of some of his friends, and he knew that at any moment his number could come up and he would never again see his family. Yet here he was, saying it's not depressing?

. . .

I think … I think it is partly due to the mystique of 18- and 19-year-old men. Because you got to consider yourself macho to a degree to be in the Marine Corps. The best, the few, the proud, the brave, you know all that. So, there's a certain machismo to it. And even though we were all afraid at one time or the other at Khe Sanh, I mean terrified, you kept this up, this bravado up. I mean jokes and this and that. It was just things to keep the image up more than anything else. We were going to fight like tigers. I honestly do believe that even though we thought that none of us would live through it we weren't willing to give up.

This is the power of the group. The other Marines were not strangers. Some were Marines who went through training with him. He had bonded with them, and when the chips were down, he felt he could face death because they were all in the same boat. He often referred to these guys as his friends.

You know, I really do think that guys did what they had to do because the alternative was that you would be ashamed if you didn't. At least that's the way it was with me and the other guys in my outfit. We did what we had to do. You know, that's why I've always felt really strange about them giving me the Silver Star. I didn't do anything beyond what needed to be done. I had no options when it came to protecting my family.

Danny clearly had a strong commitment to the guys in his outfit, and knew that they were equally committed to him. When he said this, it reminded me of a person who breaks into a burning automobile when someone is trapped inside. The gas tank could explode at any moment. This hero saves the person in the car, and when praised for it says he doesn't consider himself a hero: "I only did what had to be done."

Your family?

Yeah, they made me a squad leader and later a platoon leader. The guys in my platoon were my family, and you do what you have to do to protect them. Otherwise there is absolute disgrace. There's no option there. It's not like a choice. Is it? It's not to me. It never has been.

During this initial time in Khe Sanh, were you primarily shelled by mortar and artillery?

There was only one time that we took a frontal assault, a wave, a human-wave assault on the base. And there were only about 2,500 of them that tried it. And they came at a specific point in the lines, down by the airstrip. And they fanned out from there. That was about a quarter mile from me.

But the 2,500 men fanned out so they were in front of us, but they were weak where we were. The primary point of their attack was down by the airstrip. They actually got five NVA soldiers inside the last strand of barbed wire before our guys shot them. I bet you they lost 2,000 of them.

How did it affect you when you saw your friends getting killed?

I made a real good friend when I was in Marine training and we remained together after we got to Vietnam. His name was Philippe. We got very close. We even talked about getting together after the war. I don't think I would have lived through those first weeks at Khe Sanh had it not been for him. He saved my life more than once. They told us not to develop friendships on the battlefield but...

I think it's impossible to avoid it.

...when you're under attack for so many weeks it's extremely exhausting. We couldn't see the enemy and we never knew when we might suddenly be attacked when we went on patrol. You quickly learned who you could depend on to watch your back.
Philippe and I were always together. I could sleep in a foxhole if he was there with me, and he could do the same. I got closer to him than anybody in my entire life. It's strange to say it, considering the uncertain

conditions of battle, but I thought I would live
through the war as long as I was with Philippe. And I
believe he felt the same way about me.

Most people would think that being around death would be
hard to take, particularly when you weren't allowed to get
somewhat accustomed to the war before being in a major
battle. What did you experience when you killed one of the
enemy?

Absolute elation. I'm not kidding.

Initially it sounded cold to hear him say he felt elated when
he killed another person. Many of the NVR were in their
early teens and were literally sacrificing their lives for their
cause, even though they were required to be in the military.
He goes on to explain why he was elated when he was able to
kill one of the enemy.

Elation?

Yes. You've got to put it into context. The nights were
terrible in Khe Sanh because you had to stand lines.

Lines?

Standing guard. Not only that, but every third night

you and two other guys had to go out in front of
your first strand of barbed wire and sit in a hole out
there with a scope and watch for NVA to come in.
There were three strings of coiled barbed wire around
a bunker. A contingency consisting of three Marines
would stand guard in a foxhole outside the furthest
strand of wire each night. The Marines would take a
zigzag route from the compound through the barbed
wire to the lookout post beyond the outer string of
wire. If they were attacked, those on watch would
alert the bunker and then make their way back
through the strings of wire to the compound. At that
point flares would be sent up, followed by mortar
fire.

What was the procedure out there?

Here's how it went. We would sit out there and every fifteen
minutes over the radio … you had headphones, one guy
would have that on … they would call you and ask you ask
for a sitrep [situation report]. If it was all clear, you cued your
headset twice. If it wasn't clear, you only cued once back to
them so you didn't make any noise.
And if the situation wasn't bad then you would break silence
and go ahead and start talking. They would ask what was
going on and then you would talk. But what happened was
you would sit there and you would watch for the enemy
through a Starlight Scope. On foggy nights you had to use
infrared, which wasn't near as good as the Starlight
Scope was.
At that time, Starlight Scopes were 3500 bucks apiece to
mount on a rifle and you could look with that, with the stars,

I mean it just threw up … an unholy green … bright light green, real bright showing an unearthly light-green haze over everything.

Looking through the scope you could watch an NVA come crawling up, I mean so slow—unbelievably slow. I would never have had the patience for it. I mean they would have had to cover a good 200-300 hundred yards that way. And we are talking hours here. To cover that distance at the rate they were going would take hours.

I assume that the NVA knew about your Starlight Scopes.

Yeah, they did. And they knew what we were going to do if we saw them.

What was the procedure if you saw one of the enemy crawling out there?

We would call back a situation report on the radio and they would tell us to come back to the bunker. We had mortar rounds zeroed in on all the territory around us. We would shoot up pop flares and then throw mortar rounds out and blow them up.

If they knew you had these scopes on your rifles and could see them, why would they take a chance of getting killed?

They were a formidable enemy. Remember, we're

talking about the North Vietnam Regular Army and not the Vietcong, right?

Tell me the difference between them.

The Vietcong were South Vietnamese citizens who identified with the communists in North Vietnam. They used guerilla tactics. They pretended to be your friends during the daytime and would kill you at night. You never knew who they were. But they were not trained like the NVA.

The NVA were a well-trained army, and they were extremely motivated to drive us out of the country. They knew they might die, but they were willing to chance it. You dig? Their job was to crawl up to the barbed wire and find a hole.

Every night, up along the lines all around Khe Sanh, there were some North Vietnamese soldiers killed in our barbed wire. Every night. That was a constant thing. They bombarded us in the daytime and would sneak up on us at night. If you killed them inside the barbed wire you had a good chance of getting them the next morning, maybe a single body or maybe two bodies, you know. But if you killed them on the other side of the barbed wire, they weren't going to be there in the morning—no matter what you did to try to keep them from taking the body.

Why was that?

I think there were two reasons. I heard it said that there was a religious purpose to it, but I think the main reason was to discourage us. We could never get an accurate body count because, if they had the chance, they would take the bodies away.

I assume that you had to take your turn at that outer post?

Yeah, it was just after I got to Khe Sanh. It was the first guy I ever shot from out there. You know, it was a funny thing like I could see him perfectly through my scope. What had happened was they had dug trenches that were within a couple hundred yards of where our lines were.

How were they able to get that close to you?

Because they had us pinned down behind our lines and we couldn't go out there so we didn't know they were doing it. We couldn't tell where they were because they would be on the other side of a hill. We later learned that they had a network of underground tunnels that went on for miles. At night they would come out of these trenches and crawl up to our lines and try to find their way to the bunker.
I was sweeping back and forth with my scope like this [he demonstrated] and then all of a sudden I see him. This guy was there. He wasn't there a second ago and all of a sudden he's here. Right? He had another good hundred yards to go before he would get to us.

I started watching him and watching him, and then another guy crawled up beside him and crawled away from him. I woke up the other two guys that were with me. Usually one guy watched and two guys slept. I woke them up and told them to start going back through the barbed wire. Well, I waited until they got started through the first strand of barbed wire going back, and I waited a little longer, and then I shot this guy. I could see it really, really good through the scope. And I wasn't the first one to do that. A couple other guys had shot individuals using the scope. But I knew absolutely beyond a doubt I killed this guy.

I can see why you would feel elated.

I felt really good. I mean when I got back in, I felt like I had done something really great. And everybody asked how'd you do it? How was it? You know, all the questions and stuff. I felt really good. Everybody was happy. I was really exhilarated. This was what I was supposed to be doing, and I felt great about it. And it's the same way I felt when they finally attacked us and we killed them, because we could look out there and see their bodies.
The next morning my body, the first one I shot, he was gone. Right? But I knew beyond a doubt I had shot this guy. I think it was the next day when they tried this wave assault. It was like two o'clock on a Sunday afternoon. Then we got to see them up close. And dead. And they hung in our barbed wire for two or three days.

They wouldn't let us get them. We would go out to
get them and they would shoot mortars at us or
shoot rockets or artillery at us and we had to lay out
there while they were bombarding all around us and
then crawl back in as quick as you could. Finally, we
got them off the wires but it was three days in
coming.

How did you feel after the enemy's ground assault was over?

Right afterwards?

Yes.

You know what it was? You know how you get when
you've done something really exciting and then it's
over with? You feel almost lethargic but then after a
little bit the adrenalines gone and you're really down
[laughs]. Everybody had that. But it was a kick to us
for a while, because we could see them hanging there.
We wanted to get them down from the barbed wire,
but they wouldn't let us, you know.
But that wasn't the end. The shelling and the fighting
went on for weeks. We took squads up into the
mountains in an attempt to stop their artillery. I
changed very quickly. You had to or you wouldn't be
able to handle it.

TWO

Trapped

D anny and some of his friends joined the Marines right out of high school. They were familiar with street fighting and with occasional deaths, although usually when a family member passed away. Danny didn't actually experience a violent death until he went to Khe Sanh. He had been trained to defend himself. He had been trained to kill. However, it didn't become real until he came face to face with an enemy soldier. In a war, posttraumatic stress occurs not only when a soldier sees his friends die or when he comes close to getting killed, but also when he witnesses death of the enemy.

It's impossible to describe the changes that can take place in an 18-year-old boy who sat around the dinner table with his family, danced with his girlfriend later that evening, and then only a few weeks later finds himself crouched in a trench desperately hoping that an artillery shell won't strike his position. Under such conditions, death can be seen as an enemy and as a friend, but either way it is impossible to avoid.

. . .

What effect did all that death have on you?

> I think that death, no matter what anybody says …
> from my point of view, death, especially violent death
> is something really, really profound. I don't think you
> can witness it and it not affect you. I don't care who
> you are. In one way or another if you ever do witness
> it—I'm not talking about an accident—I'm talking
> about a deliberate violent act that leads to death. Like
> somebody shoots somebody to death right in front of
> you or cuts somebody's throat, so you see it. You'll
> never forget that. You're never going to be able to
> shake that. You can put it away and maybe it will
> weaken with time but I don't think that any other
> single act that you could view would be near as
> profound on you. That's my opinion. That's what you
> experience in war.

Can a person get over it?

> I think it could be purged … you might be able to
> purge it out of someone with talk, and it might not
> even have to be the specifics of it, you know. If they
> could just relate some of what happened, you know.
> That might help purge it down but I don't know. I
> can't say that for sure because I didn't talk about it.
> What was inflicted on me in Nam I never talked
> about with anybody. You might be able to take some
> of the mystery out of it. It's a monumental thing.
> There's nothing in life that compares to death.

I've heard it said that you are never more alive than when you're close to death. Is there any truth to that?

That's been said and I believe it's so. I think it's really an oversimplification, but it is so. You are never more alive until you see somebody dead because you never really are in touch with your mortality until you see death. It's something that we let slip away from us.

How do you mean?

You know, I could be gone in a minute, but we don't let ourselves think about that. We don't say that. We don't feel that, and when we see a dead body lying there, sometimes blown to pieces, then you think about your own mortality. You know? That's probably what makes it so profound. It affects you deeply. It affects everyone's personality. I don't think that anybody can witness it, and especially you cannot carry it out, and it not affect you. I don't believe that at all. That's just my personal view but I don't think so at all.

Death is bigger than life. Death conquers life. You know what I mean? Death is waiting for everybody. It ends life. It is something that everybody gets to one way or another. It is a longer period of time.

What do you mean by it being a longer period of time?

You are going to be dead a lot longer than you are

going to be alive if you subscribe to that philosophy. Life is for seventy-plus years, death is for eternity, as far as we know it for a fact right now. That has always worked in my psyche, that death is a doorway into eternity, where life is seventy-plus years. I saw the imbalance of that in the attention we pay to life and how we try to dismiss death. Like, let's not talk about it and it will go away. At least in my family and surroundings it was that way.

౪

Were you around much violence when you were a child or a teenager?

Not that I started, anyway. I remember times when I fought a lot as a kid. In my neighborhood it was an accepted procedure, fistfights and stuff, no weapons. Usually what I would do is get another person—this was when I was a young boy—in a headlock, or a sleeper-hold-variation thing and just squeeze their neck until they gave up and the fight was over. It never was a vicious attack. I would never beat them unconscious. It was unheard of with me or my friends. Even when I got older, I'm talking about when I was in high school; it would never be more than fist fighting.

I would never beat a guy, get them down, and kick them around and do all that. I would beat them up, knock them down or something, and wait for him to get back up and finally say that he had enough. I would be careful of where I punched him. You had to be careful because if you hit a guy in the throat you or punch a guy in the nose you can break his nose off up in there. It goes up into his brain and can kill him. So, it had to be that I would punch him from the side or punch down. I had really no malice.

Were you an angry kid?

I was angry a lot because of the way my life was working out. I was a poor kid and I hated it. I hated the rich kids getting an out. It was like they had something coming because they had money and they hadn't done anything to deserve it. From an early age that bothered me that they could somehow look down at me for having less.

But I wasn't vicious. I wasn't capable of it. If you take away Nam, I don't think I would have ever killed anyone in my life and that's the truth. I can't see me doing it. After Nam and after being, I guess, desensitized to death it was different. Up until that time I had only seen people dead in a coffin. The only dead person I had really seen outside a coffin was my father and that was in a hospital bed.

And that's very different from witnessing death on the battlefield.

Yeah, that's not the same thing because violent death has its own aura around it. It's really funny 'cause I remember the first time I saw a dead body in Nam. It was an experience that would reach inside of anybody, and particularly for the guys who experienced it for the first time. Maybe it was different for the guys who experienced it on the street, violent death, people they knew or didn't know, but got to witness it. Maybe they felt that too. But I remember feeling like this sort of reached inside of me. This was profound. This was a really profound thing. It touched me somehow. It wasn't like that I was afraid of it or anything like that. It was just that this was an amazing occurrence.

You're having a difficult time talking about this, aren't you?

The feeling of what it was like is much deeper than my ability to put it into words. It was profound in the sense that it was unique more than anything else, but I have to admit that after a while it lost its uniqueness.

You mean you got used to it?

Yeah, it lost its effect. I remember one time a little later on when we killed like 100, and some of them were lying dead in front of us. They lay there most of the night, all the next day, and I sat six or eight feet away. I turned my back on them and forgot they were even there. It's probably kind of hard to imagine, but they were lying all over the place and we were eating and sitting around like it had no meaning at all. Like there really weren't any dead people lying there.

It's funny now when I think of that. Then, I didn't think of that at all. They were gone. They were wasted. It was like once you were dead you weren't there anyway. I got that feeling early in life, and later, when my friend died, I got that feeling that nobody was there once they were dead. I don't know if it was something I picked up or something my mind told me to make me feel better or whatever, but I remember thinking, in terms of him, that he's not there anyway. Just this body.

Your friend, are you speaking of Philippe?

Yeah. His death was the turning point in my tour in Nam, and the major turning point in my entire life.

THREE

The Warrior Code

When Danny was a child he lived in a rough neighborhood. He was small for his age, and his fear of getting hurt kept him within the fence surrounding his yard. His father, who was still alive at the time, said to him one day that if he didn't get out and face the world, it could affect him all of his life. Although he was still scared, Danny took his father's advice and began walking through the gate and a short distance down the street, and then he would hurry back to the safety of his home.

Danny was a quick learner. Poverty and ghetto violence taught him how to survive. His perceptions sharpened as he trained himself to watch for danger. His movements became smooth and deliberate. His cunning and his ability to think fast and respond quickly when threatened by neighborhood bullies led to victories in fights. The kids in his neighborhood and in the adjoining areas began to take note of this kid who would not back down from a fight.

When his father died, he looked to his mother and his older brother for direction, but this was short-lived. He felt his mother was too critical of him and his older brother was weak and kowtowed to his mother. His heroes became famous people he saw in the movies or read about. John Wayne did not go around picking fights, but he never lost one. King Arthur and his Knights of the Round Table were loyal, fair, and fought for justice. Sir Lancelot was fearless, pure, and extremely loyal to King Arthur—at least until he fell in love with Guinevere. Danny's favorite hero was the Samurai Warrior.

Danny assimilated the capabilities of these heroes into his personality when he was young. These beliefs would be very important, both during his experience in Vietnam and later when he would become a hitman. But his adherence to these beliefs would not always work in his favor.

It's often said that in time of war a person's religious beliefs give strength and courage. Many firsthand stories are told by veterans about how they avoided death because of a miracle that saved them. On the other hand, some lose their belief in a deity because of the suffering of innocent people; they can't understand why God doesn't step in and stop tragedies from happening. Some don't believe in any form of a deity, even though their parents were devout. I was interested in the religious and moral beliefs Danny had and whether or not they changed while he was in Vietnam.

Did you have any religious beliefs when you were a child?

> My parents were religious but it didn't make any
> sense to me. If there was a God why would He allow
> so much suffering to go on in the world? I think part
> of it had to do with the way my mom and dad
> fought, too. They would argue and cuss. They argued

at each other until late into the night. And being in a poor part of town had a lot to do with it. You might have a nice church, but they have a better one up the road. God's in it for the money. You see an Evangelist preacher driving a Cadillac. I took out a Jewish girl, and the second time I was going to take her out, her father took me aside and said, "We like you, but...."
People would preach religion but then accumulate things to show how much power they had while preaching about Christ. The rich kids talked about religion but it wasn't religion that got them their money. It was their family, and they didn't do anything to deserve it. They had things we couldn't have, so we used to punish the rich kids by stealing their stuff.

I was an angry kid then. I was into sports and that helped me prove to myself and others that I was good. Segregated kids have no way to deal with those who have money. I came to believe that it doesn't matter how you get it. It's the predator-prey syndrome. Everybody in the ghetto is a predator and everyone who comes into the neighborhood is prey. Ghetto kids believe religion is only an excuse to control the masses. The more you got the better you are, so the less you got the worse you are. You got yours, now I want mine. We beat up the other kids because of what they symbolized.

When you were young and lost your belief in God and the religion your parents were in, did you become an atheist?

That's a hard one to answer. I used to … I think probably, like most people it goes way back, and I was indoctrinated by the beliefs of … I have always been fascinated with, for instance, King Arthur and the Knights of the Round Table, and Lancelot in particular because he was … even from a small boy I was fascinated with the concepts of purity and of honor.

You know I believe possibly too, and this isn't too far-fetched for me to believe … it might be hard for you to swallow, but I believe I could have been reincarnated from a Samurai or something. Because all of their teachings have always felt so familiar to me. You know? When I was young I felt comfortable with these beliefs.

A Samurai?

Yeah

.

A Samurai Warrior?

I've always felt that. I studied about them and that became my religion.

What was there about their beliefs or traditions that led you to study them?

For one thing, it was their loyalty to their code. You know, you look at how you have to live. If you say you are going to live by your own code of what you feel is right and wrong, you have to stick by it. The Samurai were like that. I believe one of the biggest crimes you can commit is to break your code. To break your code is the worst thing you can possibly do. I know that sounds really rigid, but when you break your code you're in big trouble.

It is a hard thing to live up to. That's why most people don't do it. I think most people know in their heart what is right and wrong just as well as I do. How it gets there may be different for different people. Maybe it's God. I don't know. For me it was the Samurai.

That's an intriguing idea. You really do see yourself as a reincarnated Samurai Warrior?

It's always been a very natural thing for me to believe that.

You mentioned Lancelot and King Arthur.

They had similar beliefs. Honor and justice.

Let's assume for a moment that it's true. What things have you been experiencing throughout your life that tell you that you are a reincarnated Samurai Warrior?

> Throughout my life I have been impressed with different ideas. Sometimes we have an idea or we hear of an idea, or we are shown an idea and it seems real familiar. It feels real comfortable and it seems to fit what you believe in or of who you are. Or who you want to be.
>
> Duty has always been one of those beliefs for me. The highest concept for the Samurai is duty. Duty and honor are the same thing for a Samurai. What you have to do you do. You know what I mean? Okay, let me give you another example. Did you ever read Profiles in Courage by John F Kennedy? He said a man does what he must no matter what the personal consequences are. I think he said it was the highest form of morality. To me, that is the same thing as the Samurai's code, exactly the same. You do what you have to do at all costs.
>
> Now, to me, that is absolutely familiar and it smacks all the way back to the Samurai. There are a lot of things like that. People talk about honor and duty in the Marine Corps. There is no difference in that and having an allegiance and of showing honor and duty to my Warlord. What is the difference? It is all the same to me.

Then the Samurai doctrine is your religion.

Yes. It has always made more sense to me than Christian beliefs.

I have another question. Vietnam Veterans I've spoken with have said they had mixed feelings towards the South Vietnamese. They were there to protect them and yet many said they were angry at them. Do you want to say anything about that?

It's a funny thing. Until Khe Sanh—like I had been there two weeks before I got to Khe Sanh, right? It is strange because I had seen a guy in the back of sixteen-wheeler truck, a flatbed truck, hit a Vietnamese with a stick. I mean he hit a lot a Vietnamese with a stick. I was riding in the back of a truck with him, and we were riding along, and they were on the side of the road, and he would take this long stick with all the branches off of it—a knotty stick—and he would reach out and smack them as we went by on the truck. Or push them off into the rice paddies, even if they were flooded, or if he would see one on a motorbike, he would really get excited and he would reach out and whack him one. I remember feeling that on one hand, I shouldn't say anything to this guy 'cause he looked salty—you know? He'd been there a while. And I was brand new, my clothes were still green— they hadn't weathered yet. But I felt like this isn't right hitting old people, women, anybody, you know.

Now let me give you what happened after Khe Sanh. After Khe Sanh we were coming back. I had been through Khe Sanh and I had been through the attacks on the mountains outside of Khe Sanh. Now later I'm back in the rear on a different assignment. We were convoy security along a stretch of road that had to be cleared. The first thing every morning when the mine sweepers swept it, we walked in the paddies next to it. Once we got this done we would ride back in the trucks. We would take C-rations with us, canned C-rations. Some of them really heavy, like beef and potatoes, really heavy. And these people would line the roads begging for stuff. And we would throw these cans at them, hard as we could throw them. And if the houses were close enough to the road, their little thatch houses, we would throw right through their houses and knock them down if anyone was in there. I mean that is the difference. I remember thinking this guy hitting them with a stick wasn't quite right. I wasn't going to say anything 'cause I figured I didn't know where this guy had been. I knew enough subconsciously that I was new and this was a completely new thing to me. It smelled different. Everything was different about Vietnam than anything in America. Here it was about three months later and I'm hitting them with cans, up close, hard enough to really hurt—break bones and you know.

Why do you think you did that? After all, it seems like these people were not the enemy.

No, they weren't the enemy. But in a way they were the enemy for us. I mean it was a real love-hate relationship we had with the South Vietnamese. You sort of wanted somebody to say, "Hey, you're really great. You are doing something really great for us." See? They never did that, they never said that. So, I think that's what brought about that hate relationship.

When they wanted something it was always, "VC [Vietcong] number 10, GI number 1." And if you did anything wrong, then it was, "VC number 1, GI number 10."
They were constantly begging for a cigarette or some money or some food or something. They lined the streets everywhere you went. If you were anywhere near a village, they would come out and line it and they stood there with their hands out begging. So, it was tough to respect them, you know?
And you had this feeling that if it wasn't for you I wouldn't be here.

Once I got out of Khe Sanh I was really aware that I was more politicized on war than I had ever been because of what was going on back home and the information we had gotten at Khe Sanh about the student riots and them saying we should get out of the war and all this shit. And all these things they were saying that we were doing that we weren't doing as far as I could see. I'm not saying that some of that wasn't done, but I think it was blown way out of proportion. I still do as far as women and children and babies getting killed in Vietnam. Like we just did nothing but kill civilians.
You know, there is a point to be made here, too. There is a certain amount of frustration involved when you are in a firefight and they take the bodies

away. It was a good psychological move on their part. When you are in a firefight and you see your guys around you that are dead and wounded and when you don't see their bodies it works against you. They really, really tried all the time to get them. Everybody was kind of hip to what they were doing. It wasn't like we didn't know what they were up to, but still it was frustrating.

FOUR

The Death of Philippe

Keeping the airstrip at Khe Sanh in a usable condition was nearly impossible. The landing strip was torn up by continual bombardment, and the Marines would try to patch up the holes, only to have new ones made by mortar shells. It became too dangerous for aircraft to attempt to land, so supplies were dropped by parachute as the choppers flew over the area.

The Marines were exhausted from lack of sleep and from stress. The unending bombardment by the enemy was overwhelming, and it resulted in a belief that they would die there. Some of the Marines made death pacts. Such a contract was not a casual agreement based on brief stress. It took place only under intense emotion and anticipation of possible imminent death. With thousands of the enemy all around, and only a handful of soldiers to fight them off, it was a desperate attempt to avoid thinking about what the enemy might do to you if they captured you.

Danny grew up in a poor neighborhood. He lost his father when he was young. He wouldn't allow himself to grieve over the loss of his father, and yet grief and guilt would haunt him for the rest of his life.

Even though he didn't see a lot of examples of it in his neighborhood, he believed in honor, duty, and bravery, and he became attracted to the beliefs and traditions of the Samurai. His conviction that he was a reincarnated Samurai Warrior became his reality. The Samurai teachings became his religion and continued with him throughout his childhood, through the Vietnam War, and throughout his life as a biker. The belief eventually allowed him to feel justified as a contract killer.

Danny was a fighter when he was growing up, but not a vicious one. He believed that an opponent should never be hurt in a fight more than what was necessary to end the fight. He was always against the bully who picked on the little guy. He believed strongly in eliminating injustice, but he had his own definitions of justice.

This next part of his story was difficult for him relate. The only other time that he experienced this much emotion in talking about his life was when spoke of unintentionally killing that young boy as a professional killer.

Some people go into a war with a macho attitude about their willingness to die for their country. When you believed you were faced with the probably of dying there at Khe Sanh, did it change your moral beliefs? It must have been extremely traumatic to face death.

> You know it was ... I think because it ... I think it was a collective thing. Nobody would let you. You know what I mean? Everybody was in the same position. I think we all ... I know for a fact we all faced that by the fact that we had death agreements.

. . .

Death agreements?

> Practically everyone had a death agreement with
> whoever they were closest to. If I am wounded, don't
> let me be taken. If they overrun us, I want you to
> shoot me. I won't let them get you and you won't let
> them get me. Everybody had those sorts of agree-
> ments. If you're making that sort of deal, you've
> already passed that point of being afraid of death. Do
> you know what I'm talking about?

You had that agreement with someone?

> Yeah, I did. Philippe and I had a death agreement. If
> it came down to it, and one of us was wounded and
> the enemy was overtaking us....

All right. I think I understand. Tell me more about Phillipe.

> Philippe was a real close friend, somebody I cared
> about a lot and … I got to actually see it happen and
> … I was never really the same. I had seen dead
> people before but it was … not the same.

How did it happen?

We ... we were in a bunker and the NVA were all around us. We had strings of barbed wire around us so that if they rushed us, they would have to go through the wire before they could get to us. And we had land mines in the areas between the wires. There were three sets of these barbed wire barriers, and there were openings where we could get through. We knew where these openings were, and they didn't. We continued to have sentries who would stand watch in a foxhole outside the perimeter at night.

Did something happen?

Yeah. This one night ... a guy was assigned to be on watch. But ... he said he was sick. Philippe volunteered to take his place, and ... he went out there and ... and ... he really didn't have to go out there that night.

If this is too difficult for you to talk about right now, we can come back to this when you feel you are ready.

No, that's all right. I don't talk about this very much because I've never handled it very well.
We had taken one hill and had moved in place for an assault on another hill in the morning. There had been a lot of fighting for the past several days, and Philippe had saved my life on more than one occasion.

. . .

But something happened.

> Yeah, it did. It was just after midnight, and Philippe clicked his hand mike, indicating that something was coming down. The men in our bunker were put on alert for a possible attack. He sent the other two guys who were with him back first, and then he was to follow.
>
> I had a bad feeling about this. The SOP [standard operating procedure] was that there would be radio silence unless there was an attack. But if the enemy is running towards you, radio silence is a useless waste of time. You yell "attack" into your mike and get the hell out of there.
>
> Philippe yelled into the mike that we were being attacked. He could see it through his Starlight Scope. We were to wait until all three guys got back to the bunker before we were to start firing.

What went wrong?

> I don't know for sure. I don't know if the NVA fired first or if one of our guys did. But there was an explosion. A bullet had hit a land mine, and Philippe was still out there. I ... I heard him scream and ... I knew he had been hit. I jumped towards the sandbags and started climbing out of the bunker. The other guys grabbed me and held me back. They threw me down on the ground and held me there.

. . .

You thought you could have been able to help your friend?

Yeah, I did. I wanted to kill the guys who were holding me down, but I couldn't move. I think there were four of them on me. Philippe just kept screaming. The North Vietnamese didn't kill him. They let him lay there … dying. He screamed for me … he screamed for help from me, and I couldn't go to him. I'm sure it took only a few minutes for him to die, but it seemed to take forever. I knew that if he didn't die from his wounds that they would kill him in the morning. They were just waiting for me or someone else to try to save him.

I assume you were aware at the time that had you tried to go out to him both of you would have been killed.

I knew that. Yeah, I knew that but it didn't matter. He had risked his life to save my life and now I couldn't do anything to save him. There was some shooting on both sides at first, but it stopped. Our guys were behind the sandbag barrier and the enemy was out in the bush. They knew where we were but they couldn't get to us. We knew they were out there but we couldn't see them.
The shooting stopped, and it was very quiet. We and the enemy laid there waiting for something to happen. But nothing happened. Philippe's voice got softer and softer. I laid there hoping that he would die. I pleaded to hear a shot from the enemy to end

his suffering, but it didn't happen. That sounds funny. I didn't believe in God, yet I pleaded with Him to let Philippe die to stop his suffering.

I could feel Danny's sadness as he related this story, but what I felt must have been mild compared to what he was seeing and hearing in his mind. How many thousands of times over the past twenty years had he re-lived sitting in the bunker that night, knowing that he would hear the voice of his friend calling to him and that he wouldn't be able to save him? Would he ever be able to shut off the terror and guilt he had felt that night? I had no doubt that he loved this friend as much as he had loved anyone in his life. Beyond that, he had made a death pact with Philippe, and he had failed.

Danny continued:

Then it was over. I knew he was dead but I could still hear his voice in my head pleading for my help. I went out at daylight when we felt the enemy was gone. I was the first one that got to him. The explosion from the land mine had blown his legs off. They had taken his boots! They took his boots off his legs and kept them!

Why do think that taking his boots bothered you so much?

Because they had not only killed him, they defiled him. For some reason, taking his boots bothered me more than the fact that they killed him.

. . .

Is that what bothered you most about that night?

> No. I think that what bothered me the most was that
> they ... they let him die slowly like that.

Is it possible that what bothered you most was your guilt? He
was a close friend and he protected you, but you couldn't do
the same for him. You had a death agreement with him, but
you couldn't honor it.

> That's true. I have never been able to get over that
> guilt.

Can you recall the changes it produced in you?

> Well, immediately it was ... I was like ... really
> agitated and really angry and I think I was afraid to
> ... I was really afraid and ... later on, I'm talking
> about hours later, it was like I was numb and I was
> standing outside of it, of what was actually going on.

Derealization is the experience of being detached from
yourself in the face of extreme trauma, a sense of being
outside your surroundings. Everything seems unreal and
dreamlike. In Danny's case, the trauma was not just
Philippe's death; it was an accumulation of the nonstop

bombardment by the enemy that had occurred since he got to Khe Sanh. Danny had seen others in his company get killed, but Philippe had been his primary link to staying alive.

How do you mean?

> It was like ... for some reason or another I had ... I ... I had ... I just quit feeling it and it was like ... like he wasn't ... he wasn't there anymore. And it might have been something to do with ... him getting ... actually touched by the North Vietnamese soldiers.
>
> I got old quick after that. The rest of the time I was in Nam, and the rest of the time in life I ... from that moment on I never did really feel it ever again. It was like a one-time affair. We're only talking about hours here, a couple or three hours, and I didn't feel it anymore. It was like I didn't feel anything ever, and I'm just getting around to feeling things now.

What effect do you think Vietnam had to do with what you became later?

> It was utter and absolute. There is no way that I would have been capable of doing what I did if I hadn't been in Vietnam first. I had been in other violence but it had been fistfights; it was never more than it had to be. You know what I mean? I had never fought to hurt anybody more than they had to be hurt. Nam changed all that.

Philippe's death changed the direction of your life?

> I was numbed by it, and I never ever, ever the rest of the
> time I was in Nam, felt anything remotely close to that.
> And I saw a lot of guys killed. Nothing at all like that.

What do you mean you didn't feel anything? How about
happiness or anger? Or depression?

> There were only two emotions that stayed with me, and
> they have stayed with me forever. Anger and depression. I
> could laugh and I could smile, but I was never in touch
> with what was going on. I understood the emotional things
> on an intellectual level but I didn't feel them anymore.
>
> I didn't have any feeling for the people I had really
> cared about. Like people like my mom and my brother and
> the other people in my family. It's like there was just some-
> thing off center, a connection that wasn't made. Ever again.
> I never ever really could, and I kept wondering if I was
> insane. I knew what was supposed to be, that I was
> supposed to feel from the heart.

What electrochemical changes occur in the brain when a
person is subjected to overwhelming trauma are for future
research to determine. That there is some alteration in the
functioning of the brain under these conditions is indis-
putable. The fact that combat veterans continue to re-live the
trauma twenty years or more after the event, and some
commit suicide because they can't live with their guilt, indicates the permanency of the brain alteration.

. . .

How did you handle that?

What I did do? I over-compensated for it. I felt I was lying
about the love I was supposed to feel. And that goes for my
relationships with women after that. I never could love like
you've learned about and like I've read about. It was always
exciting for a night or two, and then it was only comfortable, but not exciting any longer. The least little provoca-
tion on her part and it was over.

You're talking about after you got home from Nam?

Yeah. I never had a lasting relationship with a girl
after Nam.

Did your thinking processes change after that event?

I thought, I … up until that time in Nam I was fearful of a
lot of things. There's a saying that you either get killed in
the beginning or at the end of your tour in Nam because
you're too careful both times. I was fearful in that regards.
It was an abstract kind of fear when I first got there, but I
don't ever remember ever again feeling fear in my life. I felt
excitement instead.

What do you mean?

In retrospect, in times when I really should have felt fear, I felt excitement. There was no nagging fear like some of the other guys had. I didn't think in terms of, like, I could die or this could happen or that could happen. I felt in terms of, like, a ride on a roller coaster. I was excited about it, like something good was going to happen. I was excited in that regard. I wasn't afraid. I wasn't afraid.

I think maybe too, I don't know, but maybe I was looking to die so I wasn't afraid of it. Like I was looking forward to it.

Were you self-destructive?

Yeah. Everything about my behavior from that event [Philippe's death] to the present day has been self-destructive. I got into drugs in a big way. I'm talking about narcotics and heroin. I got into motorcycles and motorcycle gangs. I did crazy things.

FIVE

Pathological Change

I n addition to derealization, Danny was experiencing depersonalization (the experience of events happening apart from oneself). What he saw, what he felt, and what he believed changed dramatically. Danny would never be the same as he was before Philippe's death. Yet these changes in personality were about to make him an effective leader.

With the death of Philippe, he faced the same mental challenge to survival that he had faced when his father died. He dissociated from the conditions of the war. Prior to Philippe's death, he had been cautious because he didn't want to die. Now, the fear of death was gone. Perhaps his more aggressive attitude was a subconscious wish to die and get it over with. Or maybe he believed he could be more successful in killing the enemy if he was more aggressive:

It wasn't long after Philippe's death that I was made a squad leader. We were fighting in the mountainous areas around Khe Sanh and the A Shau Valley. We would take a hill and the NVA would take it back and then we would take it again.

Did you have any nightmares or did your fantasies or daydreams change after Philippe was killed?

I dreamt very little. It's funny, but in retrospect I think everything was a dream. I dreamt all the time. I dreamt so much that I didn't dream at all, you know what I mean? Everything was dream-like. All the time. Everything was mystical.

What do you mean by mystical?

I was so far removed from the actuality of the day-by-day stuff that—and I mean this—that I had a sense that I was … omnipotent … I was almost omnipotent. Like they did not have a chance. I was not going to die. I didn't fear that at all. They did not have a chance. It was just a matter of time that if they got close to me they were dead, and I was going to kill them. I was the squad leader and I never thought in terms of my guys getting them. I was going to get them. It was never we will, it was I will.

It was like they didn't have a chance. I was not going to die. I didn't fear that at all. It was just a matter of time that if they got close to me they were dead.

What would you experience when you were going into an area where you thought you would come in contact with the enemy?

I would walk point.

I thought a squad leader was not supposed to walk point. Being in front of your men greatly increases your chances of being the first one killed in a firefight.

That's true, but I felt that I could never walk into a trap, and for one reason or another, it never did happen. When we were coming into something, it was that feeling … I'm having a hard time describing it … it was a feeling of real heightened awareness. It was excitement. Real excitement. I knew it was coming and they [the enemy] didn't know it was coming.

I stepped into a whole squad of them washing up in this little creek. They were filling their canteens, combing their hair. I stepped right in the middle of them. Within fifteen yards of me there were eight or nine guys, and I reacted first. I just started shooting. It was the strangest thing. They gave me a Silver Star for that. It was the strangest occurrence you can ever have.

Can you talk for a minute about the dream quality of it all, like you were saying?

You know what it was? First off, I had a feeling of real peace. I mean real … confident peace. You know what I mean? I knew … it seemed like … I was not afraid.

. . .

When would you feel that?

> All the time. I felt that all the time. Day in and day out. I'd
> wake up feeling physically good and I'd feel peace … what
> I'm talking about is I'd pull leaches off me and shit but I'd
> really feel peace.

This degree of change in his personality is difficult to explain.
Danny didn't know at the time why he had changed so
dramatically. Even in hindsight years later, it was difficult for
him to fully understand the change. It wasn't like he could
ask of himself, "Wow. I have really changed! I wonder how it
happened. I'll have to think about it and see if I can figure it
out." He wholeheartedly accepted this change, believing the
outside world was different.

Later in an interview, when we were talking about his life
and personality as a biker, I asked him if he ever felt that
there was more than one of him. He said he had felt that way
since he was in Nam. One side of his personality was passive
and had difficulty making decisions, but the other side, the
one he called "Charlie," was confident, a leader who made
decisions easily. It's possible that his personality began to split
when it was fractured due to a combination of exhaustion,
the trauma of Khe Sanh, and Philippe's death.

Danny continued:

> It was like I wasn't a stranger. I was not a stranger here. The
> smells were natural smells to me. I remember months earlier

when I had just gotten there. The smells were so foreign to probably everybody from the West that was over there. But all of a sudden everything was so different. It was like I belonged there. The surroundings were so natural to me, and there was no distinction at all between me and them.

His statement of "All of a sudden…" suggests that these changes occurred rapidly rather than over a period of weeks or months.

With some combat soldiers, one of the characteristics of derealization is visual distortion:

Not only that, at times it felt I was outside my body, watching over things. I had the impressions that I saw things that nobody else saw. I looked over the land and I saw everything. I saw everything all the time! I didn't miss anything! And I really honest to God felt that I smelled them. Actually, we were the ones who smelled different. They didn't. They smelled natural to their surroundings. We didn't.

But I felt I could smell them. I could feel them vibrate the air. I knew where they were. I knew when they were there, and I knew when they weren't there. It's weird. It's really strange. It's almost psychic. I swear it's the truth. I felt that.

And you know something? I didn't take it like this is really strange. It was the most natural thing in the world, and I had never really thought about it until we started talking about it in therapy. I think I had pushed this out of my mind, and when I started getting it all out I found it hard to believe it was that way. I believe there are a number of combat veterans that are that same way.

At times persons who dissociate during trauma describe it as if they separated from themselves and were above or to the side, watching it happen. This is a protective process the mind sometimes uses in an attempt to help a person survive trauma. I asked Danny if this was what happened to him:

No, not at all. I didn't have that experience once. It's like I'm in a conversation, but I'm looking over here at a place that I can't actually see from where I am. In order to see that area, I would have to climb up on something to look. I could sense where they were. People would be talking to me and I wouldn't hear them.

At this point, my intent was to change the direction of the conversation and have him compare his personality when he was in Nam with his personality when he got back home. However, he wasn't finished talking about Nam. And he was not only reciting history, he was re-living it by bringing to the surface deep memories that had been buried for many years. He was trying to understand it as well.

Compare yourself to who you were before going to Vietnam and after. How were your emotions and thinking different?

I was completely different. In one primary way, however, I was the same. I was faithful and loyal to my friends before I went to Nam and I had made my family the dominant part of my life. The thing of most concern before Nam was my family.

My family was replaced in Vietnam by Philippe. Then, after he was killed, I transferred that to the people in my squad. Their lives and their well-being were the most important thing. Nothing else mattered. In that regard, things were the same before and after the war but other than that my behavior had turned absolutely pathological.

Pathological? What do you mean?

It had to be so. I can understand it in retrospect. It had to be so. I had certain things I did because I wanted certain things to happen. You know what I mean? So, I did things this way, had to do things this way, all the time. Everything else except the loyalty thing I had before that—and even that was heightened. Everything else was completely different. I was nothing like I was before going over there.

What do you mean you had to do things in a certain way?

All of my focus and attention was on finding the enemy. I stopped writing home, and when I'd get a letter I'd keep it for a month or two before I'd open it. It seemed that this that I was doing right now was the only important thing and everything else didn't exist anymore. I'd get letters from my girlfriend, and I'd think she was a real bitch who would probably run off, and I didn't answer her letters. I had no concept of her at all. None. I'd smell her letters and get some sort of feeling of perfume and I'd think "white woman," and that would be it. I was completely out of touch. Nothing existed except the moment.

In what way did you transfer your loyalty to your men?

When I was made a squad leader I wanted to protect my men. That was part of my Samurai beliefs. If I walked point I could get one if I saw one, but I was also protecting my guys. I would protect my guys, but I wouldn't protect me. I would risk me but not them. It's like they were somehow not involved.

I was deadly serious about things. Everything was really serious or it didn't matter. I could laugh when it was laughing time, but any other time it was deadly serious. One morning I was to take my guys on patrol. I told the guys not to eat breakfast. We would take C-rations. One guy disobeyed my orders and went to breakfast. I almost beat him to death. It was that serious.

What did he do?

He kept us waiting fifteen or twenty minutes while he went to breakfast. That breach was serious enough I would have beat him to death had not the others stopped me. I was beating him with a dog chain. I would have killed him with that dog chain because I would never have been satisfied that he had been beat enough to learn his lesson.

To me, any breach of an order was absolute. I never rationalized anything. It was this way or that way. If it was this way, you lived. If it was that way, you died. Everything was in terms of life and death. It was life and death whether he ate breakfast in the morning.

What was so bad about what he did that caused you to see it in terms of life and death?

If he did it then, he may do it another time. He does not listen! One time you mess up and you'll never do it again. He does not understand what we are doing! If we are out in the bush, and I tell him to stay and protect this guy, maybe he will run off. Maybe he will make up his own mind. No! no! no! no! You mess up one time, and you'll never have the chance to do it again. Never again! Lucky for him, he got transferred out of our squad. If he hadn't, I would have killed him. I would have killed him the next opportunity when the bullets flew. I would have put one in him. Just because I wouldn't chance him.

He was putting others at risk.

The way I saw it he was putting himself at risk. I gave the orders. When the shit hit the fan, nobody spoke but me. When the bullets started flying, nobody said nothing but me.

I'm the one that hollered, "You do this, you do that, you go there." I'm the one that did all that. Nobody else! Either you listen to me or you die. It's as simple as that.

Later on, the guys in my squad that watched me day in and day out knew that I had been here for a while, and the ones that came later didn't. I overheard them talking one night about how I had been in this battle and that one. It was a respect thing, and it didn't just apply to me. They knew that I meant what I said. They trusted me to keep them alive. If you were alive after six to eight months, you had a certain amount of respect coming, and anybody that had a little bit of sense realized that. "Hey, somehow this guy has kept himself alive for six months. I'm going to watch what he does." If you were alive after six to eight months you had a certain amount of respect coming, because most of them didn't. Two thirds of them were shot, dead, or wounded.

A Marine's time in Vietnam was not only fighting the enemy. There were times when they could go to Saigon to get away from the war. The mind can't handle non-stop war. I asked Danny if there was there anything else that gave him a sense of enjoyment or excitement:

You know, the only thing that gave me a sense of excitement was killing. There had to be firefight. There had to be bullets being shot. Artillery wouldn't even give me the same kick. That's funny because incoming artillery and mortar fire coming on top of you is terrifying to a lot of people, but it wasn't terrifying to me.

. . .

Was there any feeling of conquering death?

> I don't think so. Actually, it was just the opposite. I think I was recognizing my own mortality through the whole thing. Every time, it was something that would come home to me—every time—that I can die too. That's the truth of it. I realized every time that I could die.

Something interesting had taken place. Other combat vets have had the same problem when attempting to describe death. There were times that he spoke of death in terms of his mortality. This was not a philosophical issue; it was deeply personal with him, and he had a hard time explaining it:

> I don't know why it is that I quit feeling it after that. I think what it was, was that there was nothing I could do to stop it. It sounds strange as to why I didn't think of that before, but I never did think of that before. I always thought I wouldn't get killed for one reason or other.

When you thought during those times that you could die, did you feel any fear?

> You know, there was never, from way back in the beginning of Nam, after the night that my friend [Philippe] died there was never ... anything ... about ... I was never afraid of

death … from that day on. I really didn't think I could be killed—I really didn't think so—ever.

You find me an eighteen-year-old boy out there that can envision his own mortality. I don't care what you train him to do, until he's actually involved with it, he doesn't believe it's so. He doesn't believe a [football] pass will carry fifty yards until somebody throws it. You know what I mean? It's the same thing. At first I was afraid of death. I was afraid of dying. I knew that people died in war and I had the chance of doing so and I was afraid. After the night Philippe died it was never the same. I never feared it … ever again, and I still don't fear it. And I don't know really why.

You used the word *omnipotent*.

Yeah. Before Philippe died I don't think I felt omnipotent. I just felt lucky as hell. I just felt it wouldn't happen to me. I was up on all these combat tactics. I would do the best I could do—as if that would help.

After he died I realized there was nothing I could do about it, so what the hell. I spent a long night thinking about that. There was nothing I could do to save his life. There was nothing I could do to save my life. If you're going to go, you're going to go. I became really fatalistic after that in regards to death. We are all going to go. That sort of thing. The best you can do is to pick the time and the place yourself, and that's at your own hand. Anything else is up to chance.

By mentioning picking the time and place of one's death he was alluding to something he would talk about later: planning his own a ritual death after the manner of the Samurai.

It's difficult to explain to someone if they haven't experienced that.

In the same regard there's no life without death.

This was a very perplexing statement. Granted, death comes to everyone, but I didn't think that he meant that. It appeared that he had a love-hate relationship with death. He doesn't want death right now, yet he wants to get as close to it as he can. Why?

It is difficult to explain. If I only had an orange and it was the only piece of fruit I had, how could I explain an orange? What do you relate an orange to if there are no tangerines? If there's no lemons? You know what I'm talking about? That's the situation you have with death. That's what you got with murder because, from my perspective, nothing, nothing is even close to being a more profound experience. There is nothing that compares with it.

That might be my own point of view. It is my own point of view, and I don't know if anybody else has ever thought that or read that or what the hell else. For me, and I've had a lot of life experiences, there's nothing, nothing that will undo that. I've seen people OD [overdose] and die on drugs, and it was not the same thing. Not the same thing at all.

What if you had been the one who caused the overdose?

Maybe. Now that's different. If I would have done that that way? Hmmm. That's interesting. I still don't think I would have felt the same degree of importance or intensity or....

Sense of power?

Yeah. I saw people OD on drugs or saw them immediately after they OD'd on drugs. It seemed to be such a sneaky way to die, to slide out of life. They didn't even know they were going. Nobody else around knew they were going. It's like it slipped up on them.

The thing about violent death is that right before the instance of somebody killing you, if you see them and you know it's going to happen and you can't do anything about it. There's something profound about a face-to-face killing of a person. I think there's something that happens to human beings when they are about to die. I don't believe that your life flashes in front of you at that moment. That would be the fastest flash in history of anything. In violent death you don't have time for your life to flash in front of your eyes.

How long have you been thinking about this?

It started when I was in Nam. Everything was changed by that one event alone.

When you say that one event, you're talking about Philippe's death?

Yeah, and it wasn't so much ... I mean it was the fact that he was dead but death isn't an ending.

I don't understand. You've been telling me about how you changed after his death yet you say it wasn't so much. What do you mean?

I still don't believe death is an ending of anything. I don't believe in heaven and hell, but I don't believe death is an ending to anything. It doesn't make sense to me. Things change and things are different when you die, but it's not ... that's not an end to anything but this existence right here. I don't by no means believe this is the only existence there is.

With Philippe, it wasn't as much that he was dead as it was the circumstances of his death. I think probably the only time in my life when I've come close to grieving like other people grieve was at that time. I felt somehow that ... I should have been able to do something about it and I couldn't. Not only that but I had to watch it and ... it affected me ... me in a way that I wasn't really ... ready for.

It was like I couldn't really ... by the time I got to see him—and it was morning and we are talking about a period of maybe five or six hours that ... I was numb to the fact that he was dead anyway. I had already worked it out in my head that he was gone. They had killed him, and I knew that they had touched him. So, when I saw him I didn't feel anything but hatred. And a lot of it. It wasn't like … it wasn't even anger anymore, like how anger has always been a hot emotion with me. This was a cold emotion … more of a hatred is what I call it.

A deeper emotion.

Yeah, it was, and for some reason it wasn't just … I don't think it was just focused anymore. Well, at the time it was. It was focused on the Vietnamese. I mean Vietnamese soldiers and stuff. You know, it was focused on them. I did everything in my power within the next immediate couple of months that we were on that operation—I probably killed … I don't know … probably about twelve or thirteen people in that length of time. Vietnamese soldiers. I had absolutely no feeling with it at all … attached to it. I could have been doing anything. I really could have been. But … there were six more that … that really had nothing to do with it.

Six more? What do you mean?

I murdered those six.

SIX

The Six

On one operation Danny's company were under siege by a large number of the NVA. The marines had taken a hill and the NVA retook it. The marines attacked the hill again and recaptured it. The fight had lasted for days. Danny's company was depleted. They had lost a large number of their men including many of their officers. They anticipated that they would be replaced with a fresh company. However, it didn't happen until they had lost so many men they had lost much of their effectiveness.

> We were on this one operation where the NVA attacked us.
> It went on all night. By the time we came off that operation
> I had killed 12 for sure but maybe 18 of the enemy.

In the morning he was asked to take his squad down through a ravine to search through the bodies of the enemy to check for any who were still alive. His men went down into the ravine ahead of him and by the time he got down there they had located six enemy soldiers who were wounded but were still alive. Danny had his squad position the enemy soldiers kneeling on the ground next to each other. He walked in back of them. He shot and killed each one. His actions were impulsive. He executed all six of them.

> As soon as I was told to take my squad out there and go through the bodies I think I was planning on killing anyone who was still alive. This was different from what went on during a battle. This was more... like in later years I would come to think of this as murder more than as war. In fact, it was murder. I believe it was the first time that I ever murdered anyone that I could say that I murdered them.

Danny had killed a few of the enemy the day and night previous to this event. As he talked about killing the six enemy soldiers his demeanor changed. He looked down, he struggled to find his words and I could see that telling me about this was painful. This was the first time he had spoken of this to anyone.

> That didn't do it.

It didn't do what?

I was killing everybody for Philippe more than to protect myself. The thought of protecting myself had went somewhere the night he died.

I had them all lined up on their knees and I looked at them for a little bit, you know, maybe a couple of minutes. I just looked at them. I wasn't hot angry. I really wasn't hot angry. I didn't think at all that this would take care of what they had done or what their peers or cohorts had done. This would not do it. This would not do it. I knew it at the time that this would not do it.

Not do what?

That this would not get back at them for what they had done to my friend. It was like I was cleansing myself somehow, in some way, trying to.

Cleansing yourself from what?

Cleansing myself from the anger I had against them for killing Philippe.

It was strange because I just walked up beside them to where everybody was lined up. I'm talking about the prisoners, and I just started shooting them. I saw them but I didn't really hear them.

Do you think you could have stopped?

No. No because actually to be honest from the time I started until I stopped, I don't remember that middle group. I remember... it's like... it's like there was only one but there were six. They are all the same in my memory. I don't have any specific recollection of the others. In my memory it's like there was one.

How did the men in your squad react to this?

The guys in my squad were shocked by it. Actually, they were stunned by it. Nobody said anything. I looked at them and I turned away and I was picking up my stuff. And when I looked back these guys were ... my guys ... were taking their stuff. And then I really freaked out. My guys had pictures and everything. They were taking all of their stuff out of their pockets. I screamed "No!" at them and ran back at them and everybody threw what they had down and started backing up the hill. I pointed my pistol at them and I told them "I'll kill you." Our whole relationship changed on that.

Why didn't you want them to take the stuff?

That is exactly what had happened to my friend. They had taken his stuff. They had taken even the boots off his legs.

These were enemy, and you still didn't want it to happen to them?

I didn't want it done in the same way. I mean death is one thing. I think more than anything it was the similarities of the situation... um. Even though they didn't kill my friend, that is they never shot him, they let him die because his legs were blown off and he died that way. But somehow they contributed. They were the cause of his death and so I was the cause of these guys death. But I didn't want similarities. I didn't want anything similar. And somehow this made it feel like we were the same as them and it really, really bothered me. And it took a long time for me the get over it. Every time I would look at my squad, I would get this thing where I had a hell of a time talking to them.

Because they were trying to take these guys stuff.

Yeah, I think, to be perfectly honest with you, when they had their stuff in their hands, somehow this was like these are people here see; here is their watch, here are these pictures. Somehow these are people. I never was so far removed that I didn't realize that these were people, I knew they were soldiers. I knew this was wrong. You don't kill soldiers. You don't kill captured soldiers, put it that way. Especially wounded, captured soldiers. I was aware of this.

It is hard now for me to go through this memory. I was a cold, cold person. I even thought about ... ah ... I entertained a lot of thoughts at the time about like certain individuals in my squad that I might kill when the time was right. You got to remember I had just taken the squad. I hadn't had them that long. I mean I had had them a little while. Time is really compressed there. I had had them a while so that we were close, but we were nothing like we were going to be. You know as it worked out.

. . .

So, is it accurate then to say that you might not have cared that much for some of the guys prior to that? You didn't have any real thought of harming them. But after this event, then you started having more thoughts about what you might do to them.

> Yeah. I thought in terms of you know. I don't even know why. I've never really known why and I have never talked about it. They were aware of it. I think the individuals that were in question in my mind were aware that I was thinking along those lines. But everybody made an effort to um... get close. And it didn't take but maybe a week maybe a few days and we were really close. Closer than we were before.

Did it work? You had killed a number of the enemy on this operation and the night before you had killed two of the enemy. Did you feel you were finally getting even for Philippe's death?

> I didn't work. It made things worse. I got angrier. It was only a matter of maybe a minute and the whole thing was over. I got angrier as it went along and when it was all over with, I felt really, really angry. I felt really angry and I immediately transferred the anger that I felt to the people that were with me.

Why do you think you got angrier when you killed them? Why do you think the anger increased rather than decreased?

> I don't know. I really don't. I never did really understand that. I was like it wasn't enough. It wasn't enough and I knew it from the start. I knew it before! Before I started it, it wasn't enough, but it made me... it really made me angry that it wasn't enough. I don't... I don't think I had... at the time I know I didn't have any idea that... ah... it was never going to be enough. That came later. That there would never be enough. From that time on it was never enough and it... it didn't really work at all. I think... I think I was sort of like fooling myself with it. I'd get excited about it you know, but it would immediately go away. It wouldn't be long. It wouldn't last. There was no... euphoria.

You say you got excited. At what point would you get excited?

> When we would start... when we would get into a firefight or something, you know, usually in the jungle you couldn't locate them right off the bat. You were lucky if you could. Real lucky. So, it took a little time to get everything together where everybody's at, and everything. When I would get it together and I knew where they were and I knew I was ah... I knew I was going to get one of them. It's like I knew I was going get one, or I was going to get more than one, I'd get really excited. It was like something to win or something to do, like something really important.
>
> I felt at gut level that I was getting even. You know, for the loss of my friend. But it never worked. It never worked. And I was always aware of it and somehow, even being

aware of it, I lied myself into believing it was something more than it was. You know? That it was somehow working, but it wasn't working. Not really. And I kept getting more and more, what I call it, wacked out about it. I kept trying to move it onto another level. Actually, what I think I was looking for, what I wanted, was hand to hand. I wanted to kill one of them with my hands. And, I thought maybe that would help. And I kept putting myself into positions where I could maybe have the opportunity to get my hands on one of them.

Was there a feeling that if you were more violent that it would help more in relieving some of that anger?

I... I was looking for... I think I was looking for the one kill that would say, OK, it's done. You know? That somehow that... that would happen. I had some sort of notion in the back of my mind that if it could... It was a certain way it had to be done or a certain one or something. It's like an instant candy wrapper or something. That there would be one and it would be the right thing. Somehow I think... you know, and this is guesswork. I don't really remember. But at that point I think I was looking... somehow I was going to kill the one that killed my friend, you know. It was never going to happen. On another level I knew it was never going to happen. Even if it did happen, I would have no way of knowing, but I kind of had this thing that I would somehow know. I would somehow feel this, but it never worked.

Did that event with the six prisoners change you in some way?

> Yeah. I couldn't understand why I had done it. I realized it was wrong. It was after this event that I became more involved with the Samurai. That became my religion in Nam. I believed honor was an issue, a huge issue. I believe the killing of the prisoners under my care was the thing that touched that whole thing off. It made me really... like I completely... I completely divorced myself from that act, as if that act did not occur, that I had not done that. I tried to live that way, but I always had this thing, man, that I knew that I had done that. Nobody in my squad ever talked about it. We would talk about other firefights and other deaths but nobody ever mentioned that one. There were fifteen witnesses to it and nobody ever mentioned it.

Can a person "divorce" himself from a heinous act as though it had never happened? Evidently not because later in his life he felt he was haunted by the ghosts of these soldiers. He had believed in the Samurai Code since he was a young teenager but after this event he was determined to follow the Code more closely. It's if he was using the Code to attempt to justify what he had done.

An important point needs to be mentioned here. It's easy to write this event off as though it was an action by an evil person and not the product of war. Evidence throughout Danny's life indicates that he was not evil. He was not a psychopath. These types of events went on during the war, but are not things that a veteran talks about because later on when he thinks about them, he is too ashamed to speak of them.

SEVEN

Self-Destruction

W ere you self-destructive?

Yeah. Everything about my behavior from that event [Phillipe's death] to the present day has been self-destructive. I got into drugs in a big way. I'm talking about narcotics and heroin. I got into motorcycles and motorcycle gangs. I did crazy things.

After you got back from Nam?

Yeah. I was in a motorcycle club in Chicago. We used to have a bar we'd go to down by the lake. There was railroad property right next to the bar. The road would come down to the tracks and stop and there was a gate there. We used to cut the chain to get in but then they welded it shut. We cut that and finally they just wrapped a loose chain around the bars to keep it closed and we would unwrap it.

Right on the other side of the tracks was the lake, about

10 feet away. It was downhill on our side but when you went through the gate it was uphill and you would go over two sets of tracks and then you went straight over into the bay. I went on my motorcycle up and over the two sets of tracks and into the bay a dozen times. And I'd walk back to the bar and I'd be all wet and everybody would look at me and they would come and get my cycle out of the bay. I used to do that all the time and everybody would plead with me not to do it again. When I would leave the bar, they would even stand outside and watch to make sure I wouldn't do it. I'd climb on my cycle and drive towards town and they'd go back in the bar and I'd turn around and come down the hill and up over the tracks and into the lake again.

I don't know why. I don't even know why. In retrospect, there were boulders on the other side that were six or seven feet in diameter and if I didn't clear those boulders I could have been killed.

It's the same thing when I went on R&R [rest and recreation] when I was in Nam. I was in Thailand in a motel. They had a carport just under my balcony. There was a swimming pool about six feet past the carport. I got up on the railing outside my room and dove into the deep end of the pool. I cleared the carport by about a foot. These people begged me not to do it again and I'd say okay and the next morning I'd do it again. I did it every morning of the five days I was there.

Why? You were on the second story of the building. If you had slipped you could easily have killed yourself, or at least have seriously injured yourself, yet you kept on taking that chance. Why?

I didn't care. I was bored.

You were self-destructive in Vietnam yet you were protective of the guys in your squad?

Yeah. They were my family. I had to protect them. If you don't it's absolute disgrace so you do what you have to do. So, there's no option there. It's not like there is a choice. Is it? It's not to me. it never has been. There was a time I rescued a guy out in the bush and they gave me the Silver Star in Vietnam for that. It was the same way. I had no option.

What happened?

I had this guy in my squad who had been shot and he was laying out in front of me. What the hell was I supposed to do, say, "Hey, that's a bitch laying out there like that with people shooting all over your ass. But here I am behind this little knoll-like thing [laughs]." I wasn't real cool where I was at. I didn't even think about it. I really didn't even think about it. All I thought about was in terms of what is going to be the easiest way to get this guy out of there. What aren't they going to expect?

So, I moved from this spot over around to this angle, when they were thinking I was this other way. I went back in the creek and ran around just so they couldn't see me. And they were still shooting over here. And I ran right straight across in front of them and picked him up. I didn't break stride. It wasn't like they had a good shot at me. They didn't [laughs].

There was four or five of them shooting at me and they didn't have a chance. I went past in front of them so fast, they might have got one shot off. They were shooting … they still thought I was back at this other place. When I went past them, then they probably realized that I wasn't over there anymore, that I was somewhere else. They were likely asking where in the hell did this guy come from? And I was within 15 yards of them. Fifteen yards and they missed me.

You have come around the side by going up a creek and now you're over to the side and they are shooting at you thinking you are still back where you were?

Yeah, and he is laying almost directly … he is laying about three or four yards to the side about five yards. He's almost directly between me and the enemy soldiers. It was a guy named Fanua, a Samoan guy who was in my squad. they were firing directly over the top of him shooting at me. He had got shot right off the bat. See, what had happened is we were spread out. I didn't notice them at first. I noticed this one guy first and then I saw all of these guys—like a crowd and I just started shooting. Pew, pew, pew. I was moving backwards and I was moving as I was shooting. Once I shot this first one, they saw what was going on and they were trying to go up over the bank and into the weeds. They were trying to run. Pew, pew, pew, I shot, and pow, pow, pow, pow all the way around. And while I was shooting one of them had his rifle up and he was firing but he was trying to back up over this bank and he fired three times pew, pew, pew, when I fired pew. I got all the way around him and my rifle jammed up. The extractor pulled the back off the round and I was moving and turning and I was gone. I was gone. I was running for the only cover there was. It was this little bump in the ground as small as an anthill [laughs]. About two foot high and I jumped behind it. Fanua was already down.

Fanua had been shot and he was down?

The bullet wound wasn't nothing. It didn't break a bone. It went right through the lower part of his buttock. And ... I went over there and kept pulling my extractor ... when I jumped behind that little knoll. And I was hollering at him to fire and he was laying just as calm as could be, like this [demonstrates], with his head down on his arms like that [demonstrates]. He had an M79 grenade launcher, and I'm telling him fire, fire and pwech, pew, and I keep pulling on mine and I see this ripped the lip off the back of the shell and it ain't coming out, you know? So, I dropped. Then I pulled a hand grenade off and pulled the pin and threw it and goes right over there right in the creek making a pop sound. Then I pull my .45 pistol, pew, pew, pew ... fired three times and I yell to Fanua to fire.

He just raised up. The enemy by this time had come up into the weeds ... back into the weeds and was firing from the other side of the weeds right across him into me and tearing everything up; trees around where I am at and into this little knoll. And I am behind this little knoll hollering at him and looking around for the enemy, and I look at him and he looks back at me like this [demonstrates], and says, "I'm hit," and puts his head back down. And I said,

"Damn." [laughs] And I slid back down into the creek over on my side so I could stand up and they couldn't see me and I ran around here and ran right in front them. I grabbed Fanua by the back of the flak jacket as I ran by [laughs].

How many of them do you think you ran by?

I don't know … there were four of them. I killed four of 'em, including the one I shot in the chest. I don't know how many of them there were. It seems like maybe about 10, but there might have been 8. But there seemed to be a whole hell of a lot of them [laughs]. There were more than I had ever seen that up close to me. That was the closest. I had them pretty close a couple of times but not that many all at once.

You were willing to take the chance of dying to save Fanua?

I didn't even consider it. I didn't even consider it, and that's the truth. And in the situation he was in. I think … I've said this before and I'll say it again, I think you put anybody in the same situation they'd the do the same thing. I do. Because I didn't think about it. I didn't say, well I'm going to take a chance on dying to try to save Fanua. Fanua wasn't one of my favorites anyway. He didn't communicate really well. He didn't speak really good English and….

One time before this happened we were talking and he said to me he didn't belong in Vietnam. He said he looked more like one of them than one of us [laughs]. I just looked at him. He said it with such soul. If you know what I mean … such heartfelt … he wasn't trying to be nasty or anything. It was just something that had come to him. He was just sitting staring out over the jungle from the top of a hill we were on, sitting by his little hole, and I come over to talk to him. Because I tried to talk to everybody. I asked him how's it going and stuff and he just said, "I don't belong here." Which I thought was funny as hell. Like find somebody that ain't Vietnamese that does, you know [laughs]. He said, "No man, I look more like them than I do look like you."

EIGHT

Returning to War

Hold on. There's something I'm curious about. Why is it that some combat veterans return from the war and want to go back? What was it about the war in Vietnam that would make a person want to go back to it after being rotated out of combat duty or sent home?

You know, I have made this statement before and I'll say it again there was something ... I remember you asking about relief. I felt a lot of relief when I was finally on the plane and lifted off and everybody cheered and clapped, and I did too, you know. I felt a great deal of relief. Momentarily.

I felt also a sense of this isn't finished. This isn't done, that a lot still had to be done. I didn't know how different I had become to what life was like back home. Once I got back home and had this shock that I no longer felt or really behaved like I had before, even with my loved ones; my mother, my brother. Then I started feeling like I sure wished I was back in Vietnam.

It's the strangest thing. I read Phillip Caputo's book Rumor of War and in the prologue or the preface he said that he had the same feeling. He talked about how after he got home he wanted to be back. He knew how crazy that was to think like that. We think, "God I made it! I'm out of here." But it doesn't take long to want to be back. I think a lot of Vietnam veterans have that.

There were a lot of heavy psychological factors at work when we came back from Vietnam. We were supposed to forget it. But if we hadn't been forced upon to forget, we could have forgotten, if you know what I mean. If we hadn't been made to act like it didn't happen.

And I'm not saying all the vets would have that even then. But to sit around telling war stories. They probably wouldn't have. They didn't do much of that from other wars as far as I know and we wouldn't have either. But they weren't forced not to.

It is a whole different feeling, you know. The stuff I had to listen to of what people on TV and on the radio were saying about the war. Even some people I liked were saying that we had to get out of Vietnam. And that's the last thing in the world I wanted to do was to get out of there until it was over with. And I think every Vietnam veteran, or most Vietnam combat veterans felt that way.

NO! Not until we finished it. Let's win it. Let's fight them till there are no more left if that's what it takes. Because of all our comrades that had died. It's not only the ones on our side that died, but how about the 23 enemy soldiers that I put in the ground over there? What about them, you know? Why did I kill those 23 if we're going to just say boom forget it? Why did some of my best friends, people that I loved the most, why did they die there? That's the issue. And you say, well, should one more guy die for that? YES! Another 10,000 should die for it if that's what it takes. I don't care what it takes. My friend fought for something. He died for something. Bullshit! You don't say, well, we have lost enough. We have lost 58,323 and that's enough, that's the magic number, now we can stop.

The people over here thought that we were losing the war. It was a common sentiment that there was nothing we could do to win it. People were tired of war.

And I agree with you. I do. But the point is that's bull-shit. We were never losing the war. By what criteria? By what criteria were we losing the war?

You show me one war that was fought the way we were fighting it or on any grounds where we have killed 10 to 20 times as many of them and they did of us. They never held a territory for longer than a few days and then paid with everybody's life for it. You show me a war that went down like that and then tell me our guys were the losers.

It's an absurd idea. Now, if you want to say we didn't have enough guts to fight it out or maybe one more guy shouldn't die for it, I can understand people back home saying enough is enough. Because they weren't there and they don't know. Everybody in Nam and especially between 1968 and 1969, and probably before that, soon learned that it was us and only us.

What do you mean only us?

The people back home weren't on our side. Nobody was on our side but us! We quickly learned that. We were not fighting for freedom or the American flag or Suzie back home. We were fighting to survive. As a Marine in a trench next to me you were on my side and I was on your side.

That's it! Now you add the terror and death we went through at Khe Sanh then you get guys like me that feel we don't care how many more lives it took. Because it wasn't people at home that were fighting it in the first goddamn place. It was just us!

And then these people at home not only wanted the war to stop, they told us we did the wrong thing over there. They said we were fools for going in the first place. They said we should have gone to Canada instead. I listened to people that I admired and had liked at one time before I went over there shaming me for it, telling me it was wrong and that I should have known better.

After you were sent home, would you have wanted to go back if you had had the chance?

Yes, in a heartbeat!

NINE

Returning Home with PTSD

War was an experience that would put Danny on the same level as heroes from other wars. He didn't think of himself as a hero but he knew he had had experiences that very few other people have. He was worn out and ready to return to his family and his friends and to a grateful nation. He had heard of the antiwar movement but he didn't anticipate the level of hatred that would greet him when he climbed off the plane. He was excited about going home.

Danny's mother and younger brother Roy were at the airport to meet him. A few of his friends were there as well. His older brother Sam didn't come, but that was all right with Danny. He hadn't had much to do with Sam since that incident when Sam allowed bullies to beat up on Roy years before. Bullies had been harassing Roy, who evidently had some mental challenges, and Sam had simply stood by and let them accost him. Danny decided it was up to him to right this wrong, and defended Roy by fighting with the bullies. Danny won. He decided Sam wasn't honorable, and stopped associating with him.

Danny was happy to see his family and they seemed

happy to see him. However, something didn't feel quite right. Talking to them seemed different in a way he couldn't put his finger on.

His mother drove them back to their house. She seemed eerily quiet. Maybe, Danny thought, it was because Roy was asking all the questions. It felt good to be out of the war and back in the safety of his home and his family. He had left Vietnam just over 12 hours before and was ready to crash in his bed. He did so as soon as he got to the house.

He had nightmares and night terrors that first night. In the morning his mother fixed bacon and eggs, pancakes, and coffee. She was happy to have him home. Danny was happy to not have to eat C-rations for breakfast.

He felt lost that first day. He wasn't sure what to do with his time. For the past 18 months there had always been a sergeant or an officer who assigned him specific duties that he was to perform that day. He was comfortable following their orders because that's what he had been trained to do. He found himself hoping for an officer to knock on his door and give him his assignment for the day.

Danny had no immediate goals except for possibly getting a job or going to school. He still had his driver's license so he borrowed his mom's car and began the rounds of visiting one friend after another. It was good to see them, but it wasn't the same as it was before the war.

Danny said,

We came back home way too quickly. Three days after I'm firing my last bullets out of a helicopter window at A Shau Valley I was sitting at home. Three days! And I had just been killing guys in A Shau Valley. Four days before that I had killed a guy, and I'm sitting here talking to my mom and she's making me breakfast at 5:00 am. I'm looking at her, and of course she's changed in a year. Everybody seemed like they had changed. The whole world had changed. When I left everybody was a jock and when I came back everybody was a hippie in that length of time. I went into the Marine Corps in 1967, and was gone from September 1967 to April of 1969. [laughs] Hell, I was barely able to buy a glass of beer back then.

What was it like when you got home?

The kid who went to Nam didn't exist any longer. I was not that person. Even the connections that kid had, I didn't have any longer. The connections to the people weren't there. I didn't understand these people. The feelings for them were not the same. I didn't have any of that. It was like this whole thing at home was a joke.

"The kid who went to Nam," was himself. The change in him had been so profound and so complete that he spoke of his earlier self in our later interviews as "the kid." He couldn't see things the way he saw them before he joined the military. He couldn't feel about things as he had then. He expected that when he visited his friends it would be like he had returned home after having been gone away to school for a couple of years. The reality affected him greatly.

Everything back home was … was … was not only a joke, it was an absolutely ridiculous joke. It made no sense. My family were worried about things that were nothing to worry about. They were bitching and moaning about things that didn't mean a damn thing. Nothing they did, nothing they said, nothing they felt had any meaning at all!

Danny understood that he was the same way as his family and friends before going to war, but that didn't make the experience any easier. Every day on the battlefield had been intense. He didn't know from one day to the next if he was going to be the one in the body bag that night. He was committed to the war and to his squad. His focus on detecting the enemy before they could kill him was as complete as he could make it when he was on patrol or on a stakeout. He could relax a little at night, only to have to do it all over again the next day.

He continued talking about his family,

They had no commitment to nothing. They didn't believe anything really. They would mouth all these platitudes about how this is and that is and they would give all these clichés about stuff, and I could almost sit here and know exactly what will next be coming out of their mouths. You know what I mean? It's like everybody is reading from the same script and I'm reading it too and I'm reading a few lines ahead and I know exactly what the next part's going to be. It's like nothing. I don't mean that we sat around in Nam and had these huge philosophical discussions. We didn't. But when somebody said something, it was as close to reality as he could get it or he didn't say it. That's one thing about Nam. It was so damn real. And I didn't see any racism over there. Not when we were out in the bush, but I'll tell you what I did see. I saw black guys dying for white guys they didn't even know. Run out there and get blown sky high for it.

Were you eventually able to adjust?

[Laughs] No. I really couldn't adjust at all. I could fake it, though. I knew how it was supposed to be played, but I never saw the point. I never saw the reasoning for it. Why are they doing this? Why are they not being real? Why are they whining?

What was so real about Nam?

Everybody was killing and being killed. I don't think it gets any more real than that. What I mean is, you cannot kill and not be changed. You may be able to hide it real good and after a while it doesn't bother you that you killed, but I don't think anybody who has been in war can do it. On a one-shot affair, maybe. Maybe you can forgive that, but if you live it day in and day out, no, not at all.

The difference between the Nam vets and the guys who came home during WWII was that they came home to people who appreciated them having gone to war. With us it was like I had walked down to Suzie's place and had come back and I was expected to be the same. Nobody talked about it. I overheard my mom whispering in the kitchen that I had really changed. She wouldn't look me in the eye and say, "What the hell happened to you?" It was like it was such a delicate thing it couldn't be talked about. They had heard all the stuff about us killing women and children and I think she was afraid. She looked at me and saw this kid with the eyes of a hundred-year-old man. She never got over it.

In Nam I was all messed up in the head but I didn't know it. When I came home I knew that something was crazy but I didn't recognize that it was me. I thought everybody else was weird. In Nam I didn't think I was weird. In retrospect now [years later] I know I was weird and it was really evident to others, I'm sure. I was weird but I didn't know it at the time.

When I got home at first I thought that everybody else was messed up. I thought, "They've always been f-d up and I didn't notice this?" Years later, the more I thought about it, I recognized that I was the one that was screwed up. The reality was I had very little insight. Everything was absurd. None of these people are doing anything. All they want to do is bitch and whine and piss and moan about everything's that going down in their lives.

It wasn't entirely irrational that he could believe that they had changed. The clothing was different as were the hairstyles and the music. The hippy movement was strong and in a year when President Richard Nixon announced that he wanted to draft 150,000 more soldiers to expand the war effort into Cambodia, students at Kent State massively protested.

Although Danny did not like the hippie movement, this was only a small part of what bothered him.

They're acting like nobody is in charge, you know. They are telling their problem to everybody they run across hoping that somebody will do something for them.

. . .

A major difficulty he had in not being able to adjust at home was that problems were not getting taken care of. The war was still going on in Vietnam and friends of his were getting killed, and people here at home were saying the war was a mistake and that we should be getting out. He had been trained to make quick decisions because the lives of the others in his squad depended on it. The idea that the people back home couldn't make a simple decision confused and disturbed him.

He had flown out of the country of Vietnam but he had brought the war back home with him.

Instead of people saying, "I don't like this. I'm not going to let this be this way," people complained but did nothing about it. It used to drive me insane. I had no patience with people at all because all they wanted to do was complain. It seemed like everybody I ran across was that way. Friends I had were crying about their girlfriends or crying about everything you can think about. I just thought it was the stupidest shit in the world. They had no problems. If your girlfriend is giving you problems, drop the bitch and go find another one. You know?

I couldn't understand it. I just couldn't get a grip. I never really did get a grip. It was really profound. I can't say enough about it. It happened to so many guys when they came back home.

What did you decide to do?

I went down to Chicago State to live not long after I was home. It was beautiful there. In my neighborhood where I grew up, there were people who knew something about death and dying because they had lived in the ghetto all of their life. But when I went down there, here was all these rich kids who knew absolutely nothing about it the war in Nam.

They would talk about it on an intellectual level. I used to listen to them and I'd look at them when they would ask me something about the war, they were waiting for something profound to come out of my mouth and I'd say something absolutely ignorant.

Why would you do that?

I couldn't tell them about the war! How could you tell these people something? Did they really want to know? Do you think they really wanted to know? And could they understand it if I told them? Hell no! They had no idea of what it was about. They think of war as a game or something and not of killing. I don't know how we ever got away from the idea that war means so many things, grand strategies and all this stuff.

One day, Danny told me about a television show he had watched the night before. He said the purpose of telling me this story was to impress on me the point that even the generals directing the war were emotionally separated from what the soldiers out in the field were going through.

I watched this show last night about these women nurses in Vietnam. And this girl gets up. She's like a candy striper or something. She's been stationed out at this firebase with all these dudes who are really rough looking, where the infantry is at. The firebase got overrun and they had got these nurses out of there before the shit hit the fan, right?

Now she and some other nurses or candy stripers have been invited to a dinner with generals and all of these other dudes and they have all of these white women with them in this plush place. They've got lobster.

This general is talking about how the war should be fought and all this stuff about the war and she gets angry about what he is saying. She gets up and looks at him. You see, she had just come from living with guys like the general is talking about.

She feels the general doesn't understand who is really fighting the war. The people at this dinner were eating lobsters and lots of good food and the guys she was with had C-rations.

She said, "This is not your war and it is not my war. It's their war!"

I thought that was a pretty profound statement because no matter how you cut it, with war, it comes down to the guy on the ground with a rifle killing that other guy with a rifle. It's my war and it's his war. You know what I mean? It's not the general's war.

I thought that was pretty profound what she said. The generals have nothing to do with it. They just move pieces around. We don't need them. We can move ourselves around. No matter who gives the initial orders, it comes down to somebody in the firefight that's shooting the enemy with a rifle. The generals don't tell the guys in my squad what to do. I do, and these guys right here listen to me and do it.

Mine was the last order given and I was the guy who gave the order. It was that way with all the squad leaders in Nam. So, it was fought on that level. Not on some general's level. All of these grand strategies about the pacification you can throw out the window. It's us guys who are walking around with the rifles and the bullets. That's what reality is.

TEN

Constantly Angry and Depressed

D anny was back home and he was safe. He had wanted to get out of the war and yet he couldn't leave it all back on the fields in Vietnam. His mind and his motivations were still over there. His flashbacks, his nightmares, and his having been conditioned to be constantly alert and perceptive kept him on guard.

PTSD was first recognized in 1980 as something more significant than what was known as Shell Shock, which up to that point was seen as a weakness. Combat veterans with PTSD often relate that, when in a restaurant, they sit where they can watch the door. They sit in a corner or where their back can be against a wall. They are aware of the movements of others in the room. When shopping they don't want anyone standing behind them so, when they check out, they stand so they can see the people both in front and behind them.

When Danny talked about the difficultly he had trying to adjust to being home from Vietnam, I recalled what he had said about the depersonalization he experienced when Philippe was killed:

. . .

There were only two emotions that stayed with me, and they have stayed with me forever. Anger and depression. I could laugh and I could smile but I was never in touch with what was going on. I understood the emotional things on an intellectual level but I wouldn't feel them anymore. I was not emotionally in touch with people that I had really cared about. Like people like my mom and my brother and the other people in my family. It's like there was just something off center, a connection that wasn't made. Ever again. I never ever really could and I kept wondering if I was insane.

With depersonalization, it sometimes results in disconnect between events and the person's ability to feel the range of emotions usually engendered by the events. When Danny said he was "never in touch with what was going on," he meant he had lost the capability to feel nuances of emotions. It was like using a tape measure that registered only inches when one is attempting to measure one-eighth of an inch.

After Philippe was killed, Danny primarily felt anger, depression, and excitement. Anger and depression when a friend was killed by the enemy. Anticipatory excitement when he believed he was close to being able to kill the enemy, and excitement when he was able to successfully complete the act. When he was able to kill an enemy soldier, he felt satisfaction. He felt peace and then he felt a letdown when the adrenalin rush had completed its cycle.

But what is PTSD like for a combat veteran? Another Vietnam vet who took part in the skirmishes on what became known as Hamburger Hill related,

. . .

You ask, what's it like being home from the war? I have PTSD. At least, that's what they call it. However, people have a very limited understanding of what PTSD really is. They think that time and a few medications will make it all go away. They want me to be the same person I was before I joined the military. They don't understand that I will never be that person again.

There are very few things in this life that are as terrifying as looking in a mirror and realizing that after only a couple of short years the person you see looking back at you is not you, at least not the person you used to be. The outline of the face is the same. There are two eyes, a nose, a mouth. The color of the eyes hasn't changed. But a change has taken place. A change so dramatic that it frightens my family and my friends.

They know that something is wrong or missing or something, but they can't figure out what it is, and they are too afraid to ask. The softness around my eyes is no longer there. They see that, but they don't know what it means. They assume it will come back as soon as I am used to being home again. But it won't. It may never come back.

The innocence I used to have has vanished. The lines on my face are deeper, longer. My hair which was combed in such a careful manner to attract the girls a few years ago is now coarse and just seems to lie there on my head.

The thing they notice most is my eyes. Girls used to say I had happy eyes. Now they turn away because there is something about my eyes that frightens them. Some won't look me in the eye. They don't know what to call it. All they know is that something is wrong and it confuses them. They tell me it's wonderful to have me back home. They are happy that I am alive and not in some POW camp in

North Vietnam. They feel it's great that I wasn't shipped home in a casket. Still, they are not comfortable around me.

When I was a kid I saw pictures of caskets of soldiers with an American flag draped over the coffin. I was proud. I didn't know who the kid was who died on some battle-field, but that didn't matter. Whoever he was, he was a hero in my eyes. I wanted to go to war, and if my body was brought back in a casket I would be given a hero's burial. My picture in my smartly pressed uniform would have a place of honor on the mantle of the fireplace and my family would be proud to look at it when they walked past. However, I figured I would be one of the lucky ones who survived.

I used to sit on the stairs and listen to my dad and my uncles talk about their experiences fighting the Germans in France. They would get excited when they talked about how they went from city to city driving the enemy out. They laughed when they described scenes of townspeople lining the sides of the roads, cheering them as they drove by. I saw pictures of tickertape parades in New York. It seemed like there were millions of pieces of graffiti that rained down over those heroes. The soldiers were in open cars and they were happy as they waved to the thousands of people shouting and waving back.

As I reflect back on the few times I saw my dad and uncles talk about their experiences, I never heard them mention any traumatic ones. I got excited listening to Dad and Uncle John and Uncle Phillip describing their trek through France and I wanted to hear more and more. But after a while everything got quiet. Then one of them would say he was tired and that it was time to go to bed and he would excuse himself and start up the stairs. The others would soon follow. I thought it was strange that all three of them seemed to get sleepy at the same time. I understand now what it was that made them quiet.

When we came back from Nam we didn't have ticker-tape parades. We didn't have people cheering as we rode through the city. Hell, we had people spitting on us and throwing garbage in our faces when we got off the plane. If we had been able to do so we would have commandeered that plane and flown it back to Nam to finish the job we went there to do.

I can't count the number of songs that the war inspired during the 1940s but I think I could count on one hand the number of songs of inspiration that were written during the Vietnam War, if there were that many.

But wait a minute. I didn't come here to complain about how we were treated when we got back from the war. From what the people had heard here at home, it's logical that they would feel about us the way they did. It's not that they called us baby killers and they wouldn't hire us when we needed work, it's that they didn't want to understand what we went through for our country. Still, in all fairness, even when some people did want to see it through our eyes, we couldn't tell them. I didn't dare tell anybody about it and neither could friends of mine who were combat Marines.

I'm just getting around to being able to talk about it now and it's over twenty years since it happened. When I look at a picture of me just before I joined the Marines and I compare it to what I see in the mirror now, I am shocked. I am a very different person than I was. I have nightmares. I sleep with a gun by my pillow. When I go to a restaurant, I have to sit with my back to a wall facing the door. I am aware of everything around me. All the time.

There are no movements or sounds that go on around me that I'm not aware of. I had some good friends who were killed in battle. I have friends who have committed suicide. The war was horrible, more horrible that I can tell you about. Yet I want to go back, as do many of my friends. I hated it there yet I have never felt so alive as when I was over there in that God-forsaken country. Here at home I feel like a stranger among my own people. A time traveler lost in a space between reality and memory.

I have to find out what happened over there to make me change so much.

I still haven't figured it out but I won't stop searching until I do.

Being back in Illinois didn't feel right for Danny. He no longer belonged there. His home was on the battlefield where he could get an adrenalin rush by making quick life-and-death decisions. Listening to his family talk about the sprinkler system being broken or what to fix for dinner was beyond trivial. As a squad leader in Vietnam he was the one who made the decisions. There was no debate, no discussion; his decision was immediate and final. Nobody back home seemed to want to make those decisions. This was not life to him. In Nam when he put on his flak jacket he was ready engage in fights with the enemy regardless of the outcome. He had been a respected leader in Nam. Now back home he was seen as weird. He was shunned and often only tolerated.

He came back to the States without having been able to get revenge on the enemy for killing Philippe. He wasn't through killing. Killing had been associated with the hunt as well as the kill, and his life here seemed empty without it. There was nothing here for him to hunt.

He heard his mom whisper, "He has really changed." In Nam, they didn't whisper secrets. There were no secrets other than what the command wasn't telling them about the war or about their next assignment prior to the time to engage in it.

Danny had started using drugs when he was in Vietnam. He made a strong point that he would only use them when he was on leave in Saigon. He would not allow any member of his squad to use drugs when they were on patrol. Nor would he use them. But when he was on R&R he would get wasted.

Did you have nightmares or flashbacks over in Nam or after you got back home?

> Not over there but I've had a lot since I got back. But I was got heavily involved with drugs so I didn't notice most of them. Choppers going over trigger memories for most vets. And wood smoke is the thing that triggers it for me. I didn't know why but in retrospect all of their fires over there are wood fires. I hear a chopper and I immediately think of Nam and I get this apprehensive feeling.

Did you have images come back to you when you heard a chopper?

> Sure, and they are always combat images.

How real were they?

> I had a lot of them when I first got back. They were very real and for a few seconds I'd feel like I was still in Nam. I'd

have the overwhelming feeling of being in the jungle. It was like having a TV image of everybody running for cover and stuff like that. It was like the whole surround sound thing. It would last for a few seconds. It would be a complete, utterly real experience.

I'd have an overwhelming feeling of a jungle, like being in the jungle again. It wouldn't be right in front of my eyes, but the feeling was the same as when I was there. Exactly the same. I'd see a TV movie in my head, of guys running and shooting, of bombs exploding. The whole thing. I don't think any combat veteran can ever shake that. That's my personal opinion. I don't believe it's so. I can see a parallel between it and World War II on the islands. The fighting was broken down into small groups.

You mean after the initial experience at Khe Sanh?

Yeah.

So, what did you do?

I moved in with some hippies and I got into strong-arm robbery.

ELEVEN

Violence and Aggression Back Home

I came back really angry. I suppose that's a theme that's prevalent in most guys that came back, combat vets especially. I did a lot of fist fighting and drinking in bars. I was fighting all the time.

The stakes in life weren't big enough. They weren't high enough at all. And I was in the process from the time I came home until I finally got a grip on myself of raising the stakes. And that was the whole thing. Life, as I saw it around me, didn't make any sense.

W hat do you mean by the stakes not being high enough?

I mean like, life, the reason for it and how you go about it didn't seem to have enough meaning. It didn't mean anything. There was no challenge to it.

Not as exciting?

> Not exciting at all. If you ever lost, what difference does it make? You could be a bum on skid row or you could be president of General Motors. To me, neither one was exciting. Neither one of them drove me, or had any interest for me.
>
> What I wanted was something more physical, something more life or death. In reality, that's what I was going for the whole time. I was armed and I was angry.

His first attempt at work was a failure. Everything about having a boss and coworkers and working 40 hours a week frustrated him and caused him to quit. Since he had a chance to go to college on the GI Bill he decided to try that. He selected Chicago State University and took a few classes, but he was dissatisfied with the requirements of student life. He was restless and depressed, and started using drugs again. He moved into an apartment with several hippies. He didn't like hippies but at least they were more like him than the straight folk. He smoked marijuana with his roommates but it was too mild for him so he found a way to get other drugs. Even so, there was something missing in his life.

Danny got restless in the evenings and would tell his roommates that he was going for a walk. He always carried his .45 with him. One night he saw a man walking down the sidewalk towards him. When this person got a few feet from him, Danny pulled out his weapon and hit the man on the side of the head, knocking him unconscious. He took the man's money from his wallet and dropped the wallet. He hadn't planned on robbing the guy. He acted on a sudden impulse when the guy got right up to him. It felt good. It helped him to relax.

It's really plain for me to see now looking back on it that it was just a matter of time until I killed someone. That's what the whole point of it was. That's why I went out and robbed people. I didn't need the money. Money wasn't what was driving me to do it. It was the excitement involved in it. Actually, there was no sense in it. I wasn't doing it for anybody but me because nobody else knew I was doing it. It was only for me. It was the excitement of the confrontation, I guess.

He continued going out at night robbing people. At first it was on impulse and then it became organized. He did it about 20 times over the next few months.

Was it becoming an addiction? Was it like getting relief from drugs?

In retrospect I'm sure it was an addiction. It was the same sort of thing. When you don't have drugs and you're addicted to dope the first thing you start getting is anxious about the situation. Then you start thinking in terms of what you are going to do about it and then you do something about it. That's how it comes down. It's the same way, actually, to how this would come down, but it would be quicker. Because I didn't have to figure out anything. All I had to do is walk out the door and start walking and sooner or later I was going to walk into somebody. Chicago is a pretty busy town. It's pretty hard not to walk into somebody.

Drugs weren't enough for you?

I needed something more than that and, as I went along, it started out with just wild behavior, but then it became more focused with the robberies, the one-on-one sort of robberies. I was raising the stakes until it eventually led to murder. It was a progression.

Were you planning it pretty carefully?

No, not at all. To me it was like a gimme. You know, it's like it would be impossible to get caught. I had no problems with rolling guys because it had become a fact of life with me. It was part of our generation. I had no guilt because there was no finality, they could always recover from it.

You developed a habit of using violence. What did violence do for you?

Once you get started using violence to help you get through life it becomes easier and easier to do. I mean you go for it quicker and quicker. It shortens the amount of hassle you are going to have to go through to deal with an issue. It applies to anything. It is addictive. It is a narcotic.

. . .

What do you mean when you say it's a narcotic? That's a strong statement.

> It is the same thing. To me it was a narcotic because just like my addiction to heroin made it easier for me to deal with emotions, violence made it easier for me as a person to get through the hassles in life. I would use it in arguments or differences of opinions and I would use it any time I felt like it.

What would trigger violence in you?

> You know when somebody does something to you that seems inconsiderate or nasty or something, you think, "Wow, should I tell them that they are inconsiderate? I wonder if I should say something."
>
> I didn't go through any of that. What I did automatically was—boom—grab them and say, "Hey, I'll knock the crap right out of you!"
>
> When you use violence it just cuts through all that stuff. It wasn't like I would say to him, "Hey, I don't want you to say that to me."
>
> Here is how I envision the scenario. Somebody does something really inconsiderate to you, okay? An assertive person would say to him, "Hey, I don't like what you are doing. I wish you wouldn't do me that way. Don't treat me like that. I really don't like to be treated that way." And the guy says, "F___ you man, what are you going to do about it?" So, you just keep going back and forth.
>
> I would use violence or aggressive behavior from the

jump. I would slap people or punch people or grab them and tell them, "Hey, I'll kick the shit right out of you." It would cut right through all that. Because his next statement definitely wasn't, "What are you going to do about?" because I have already done it.

It just seemed to me it made it simpler. It made it easier than if I would try to work it out like most human beings do. You know, being rational and assertive and stuff. The more and more I used violence the more and more it came quicker and quicker. Less and less did I think about what the argument was about. I just automatically fell into it.

Later on, when I got in a bike club, I was with other guys who also believed it was the only way to handle things. I just believe that violence feeds on itself. You go to it more and more and more just like an addict goes to heroin more and more. It takes the place of having to deal with people on an everyday basis.

Assertiveness was one of the hardest things I had to learn in therapy. When I felt the least bit put out by something, I wanted to smash somebody. Smash 'em up. It was really difficult to change.

I remember when Kate had me take her assertiveness class. We argued all the way through it, you know? I said assertiveness was crazy. It will only work when you have two rational people doing it. But you take that crap where I am from and they will laugh at you before you can even begin to tell them you don't appreciate how they are talking to you. You'll be punched in the mouth [laughs]. They view that as weakness, absolute weakness.

Aggression had been Danny's means for physical and emotional survival since he first went to Vietnam. It kept him alive over there and he continued using aggression to fight his battles after he got home. The police eventually caught up with Danny. He was convicted of a felony on one of his robberies and was sentenced to prison.

When I went to prison I was again fighting all the time. That's what it was all about. It seemed like to me I was constantly in the process of raising the stakes in my life higher and higher and higher until the ultimate, which was life and death. And nothing else would do.

TWELVE

There is Evil in the World

Danny was able to hold his own in prison, and when other inmates threatened him he stood his ground. He was aggressive and at times violent and he quickly achieved a reputation as someone to not mess with.

He completed his time in prison. He had been awarded a Silver Star for bravery in the war but now he had a felony record which would make it more difficult to go back home. While in prison he became friends with a member of a biker club and he was impressed with the club's lifestyle. If he became a member of the club he could more easily "raise the stakes."

When he was released from prison he joined the club and got involved with trafficking narcotics. He always had a girl-friend but never got married and he didn't have any children. The club became his family.

He worked his way up through the ranks until he became one of the leaders. From then until he killed the boy he and the club were involved in a number of illegal activities including bribing and threatening witnesses who were to testify against them in court, bribing police and political authorities, and on at least one occasion bribing a judge. His club was involved in explosives and arson crimes. Not surprisingly, Danny didn't dwell on these crimes, seeing them as just part of life in a motorcycle club. But even bringing them up was a risk. I was curious as to why he would tell me about these things. He said there were several reasons. He had been in therapy with Kate and he found that he could trust that she was going to keep the information confidential. Since she vouched for me, he was willing to give me a try. We agreed that he would give me no names, dates, or places, and he said the illegal activities occurred throughout the country. He had a need to purge his soul and he trusted me—at least to a degree. He was still in full contact with contract killer friends of his who were loyal to him and I assumed that if I violated his trust … well, you get the picture.

Often, a person will talk about other people but he is actually talking about himself. Danny did this. One day he came into my office and began with:

> There is light in the world and dark in the world. Light is like good and dark is like evil. I think evil begets evil, if you know what I mean. I'm a firm believer that there is unadulterated evil in the world.

At first I wasn't clear about where he was headed with this beginning to the conversation.

> For instance, I've met people that I know for a fact they enjoy hurting other people. They are the kind of people I say come from the dark.

He went on to say that neither he nor his friends in the club had any intent to be evil and he said he was talking about a particular type of person whom he referred to as evil. Was Danny saying that he had no intent to be evil?

> You take the situation I was involved in with the bikers for instance. There is a propensity to just … act out. Act out carelessly. You know? So, you do what you want to do and the rougher you are about it, the better it is. Nobody seems to mind.

Danny acted out carelessly and he could see no wrong with it because his friends in the club were doing the same thing.

> It's part of the role that goes with being in a club like ours. Whatever one of the members of the club does was all right with the others. But when you are around those activities all the time you feel all right doing what the others are doing. That's what I mean by evil begets evil. I mean, basically, we weren't evil. We didn't set down a policy to be evil. It wasn't ever something that was thought about. You know what I'm talking about? We had other ways of thinking about it.

What was the club all about?

> It was about freedom. Freedom to do what we wanted to do. And when you have absolute freedom—and that's the only thing that we would accept was absolute freedom—doing what we wanted to do and doing it our way was the norm. That kind of breeds evil. But you've got to have some limitations, even if they are just small. If you have no limitations, you don't take into consideration how other people in the club feel about things.

Where did you fit into that? Did you have consideration for others?

You know, I really never considered, to be perfectly honest, how the squares—what we called the squares—how the squares felt about things. You know what I'm talking about?

No, I'm not sure what you mean by "squares."

Squares were the law-abiding people. When we would have some contact with them and stuff, maybe we would be rude or maybe we would cuss or maybe we would hit somebody or whatever. Did I tell you how we used to bop the boulevard?

Bop the boulevard?

We would walk up and down the streets. We would come to a section of town, like where there were a lot of pimps or prostitutes or winos or street gangs—people on the street, and we would bop. There might be 10 or 20 of us. There might be more. But, whatever, it was like a Saturday night thing like some people would go out dancing or something. We would go bop the boulevard.

What was the purpose of it?

It was just to cause trouble. We would go out and we would start to walk down the sidewalk and just chase people indoors, make people get inside. We would go into bars where we knew we were not wanted. We would hassle them at the door and maybe punch some people. You know, just to raise hell. And

… then we would chase the hookers away. We would chase the pimps away. We chased the street people away. We chased the street gangs away. We would chase everybody away.

It was like locusts or something coming in [laughs] and they knew it. It was something like a ritual or something, if you know what I mean.

Did you consider all of these groups to be squares?

All of those people were squares as far as we were concerned. They might have been a pimp or a prostitute, but they were still squares from where we were coming from. We would run them all off the streets. We would try to get a reaction and, if they would react, we would beat the crap out of them. We would do whatever it took. If they wanted to bring weapons we would come that way too. We were all packing.

But, again, what was the purpose of it?

I'll tell you what it was. It was, it was like a … a bonding ritual for the guys. I'm talking about the guys in the club now. It was like a bonding thing. We didn't have that many enemies, per se. At one time we had problems with other bike clubs but after the war with them was over we didn't have set enemies to fight. So we had to hunt them up [laughs]. We did it everywhere. See, in those days we called it bop. When you got into a fight, you were bopping. Kids today call it banging. They are gang bangers. There's not a whole lot of difference between what we did and what gangs do now. The bikers have always bopped. I don't know, we just did stuff like that.

You were talking about evil a moment ago. What do you mean when you say evil?

I've met a lot of people in my life where I can tell that … it's wild, like an insanity. They seem to have no control over it unless they are in a situation where it would be dangerous to show it. It's like they have something inside them pushing at them all the time, if you know what I mean. Something like electricity or something. I don't know what you want to call it. Something jittery, out of sync. They can be sitting there really peaceful but they still got this thing going on inside them. I've seen that and, to me, those people, every time, are people who lash out for no reason at all and they get a kick out of it.

When you say something pushing on them, any idea what that might be?

I don't know. To me, I've always thought they were nuts. It seemed to be some sort of insanity that they had that hadn't been pinpointed.

He was talking about an insanity within him and he identified this as evil. It frightened him because he had only a vague understanding of what had been happening to him. He couldn't tell me that he was evil. He could only talk about himself by describing it in another person.

He believed he had been fighting for justice, the opposite of evil. Evil was a word his Christian mother used which was applied to a person who was very, very bad. The word evil was a strong word for him to use. As in The Portrait of Dorian Gray, Danny was beginning to get a glimpse of a deeper side of him that he didn't like. To see himself as violent was acceptable, but it must have been jarring to view himself as evil and outside of his Warrior Code.

What do you think these guys would be like if they didn't have a chance to let that emotion or evil out?

> They are always going to be able to find a way to let it out. I've yet to meet one of those people who don't. They are loud and they are overbearing. When you see one that is sort of at peace for just a moment you know that guy isn't going to stay that way. The next thing down the pike he's going off on someone.
>
> I have met a lot of those kinds of dudes. I don't think it is something they can't control. Don't get me wrong. Because they can control it. I don't think it is something out of control with them at all. Whether or not they do control it depends on the situation.

Danny had talked about the anger that he had had during the war after Philippe was killed and how, when he returned home, his anger did not go away. There was no doubt that he was able to satisfy some of his pent-up aggression when he went "bopping the boulevard" with his friends, but there was something that was driving him to continually "raise the stakes." It was parallel to when he executed the six North Vietnamese soldiers during the war. As he killed each soldier in turn, his anger increased rather than decreased. Bopping the boulevard wasn't enough. What was driving him and why was he unable to understand what it was?

Were you one of them? One of those evil people?

> Yeah. I was one of them too.

What did you believe about the drive going on inside of you? What were you feeling?

I can tell you what it is. It is anger from something or other with me. It's a deep feeling of frustration and anger and ... like it electrifies you or something. You know, it's not just the feeling of anger. It's that I am anger, if you know what I'm talking about. It's not just being angry. I am anger. Period. If you know what I mean. It's not like I just feel angry. I am anger.

As I watched him, I could tell it was very difficult for him to make the point he was trying to make. He was not simply talking about a feeling or an emotion. He was talking about his identity.

THIRTEEN

Recreating Vietnam

D anny felt he had been deceived by the government, abandoned by his friends and family, and was unwanted by nearly everyone. In Vietnam he had a purpose and he was needed and respected there. At home he was lost and alone. He had developed a combat personality to survive the war but it was out of place now. He was a Samurai Warrior in an environment where there was no need for one. Like Puff the Magic Dragon, his roar was obsolete. Still, his need to fight for injustice—and for the death of Philippe— didn't go away simply because he was no longer on the battle-field. He craved the excitement and the adrenalin rush that he had when in search of the enemy. Here at home there was no enemy to hunt down and kill. Danny had a need to reconstruct a war. He was a fish out of water and he had to build a pond to get back into.

I wanted to follow up on his statement about being anger rather than having the emotion of anger and how this relates to being evil. When Danny was a child he selected King

Arthur and Lancelot as his heroes. These were characters that were viewed by many as the epitome of purity and perfection. Now, he viewed himself as pure evil. I wanted to see where this would lead.

> Every time it rained I would say that I wished it would rain gasoline and I'd throw a match out there. I felt like that. Inside I felt that people were f____ up. They were absolutely f____ up. Everywhere you turned, everywhere you looked it showed. I'd see people who were supposed to be really good and outwardly appeared to be doing the right thing and stuff. But if you look long enough you would find out that it's not that way. It's a lie. It's a trick.
>
> When I came home from Vietnam I had this terrible feeling that I'd been betrayed. I felt like we had all been betrayed and there was no way to handle it except to not get fooled again. I wouldn't let myself get fooled again no matter what they say or no matter how they act. I believed in their propaganda about the war and I got burned. I think for me that's what played into me becoming so tough. I just felt people were all full of crap and I would put them in a position where they couldn't hold to whatever their thing was, you know what I mean? I'm saying I was in the dark all the time. I chose to be there.

He and his friends hadn't been welcomed home as heroes. He watched guys in his squad who he had considered to be his family die in a foreign land, and he wanted someone to take responsibility for it. He wanted the world to be just. But what did he mean when he said he chose to be in the dark all the time? And what did this have to do with being evil?

Many Vietnam vets may have felt that they were betrayed by the government and by the antiwar movement but most didn't see themselves as evil. Many vets wanted to return to Vietnam to finish the war but most didn't feel they had to keep raising the stakes by becoming increasingly violent. Posttraumatic stress was a serious problem for Vietnam War veterans when they returned from the war and, for the most part, they had to find ways to handle it on their own. Danny couldn't find a way to do it that would be accepted by society.

Describe what it's like being in the dark.

It's like this. It's a complete life. Let's start with my attitude. My attitude about if it rained gasoline I'd throw a match out there first and foremost. That's my deep-down secret. Right? Okay, going from there, everything is centered on me. Whatever I give importance to is the only thing that has importance. I have to make my own judgments about all these things because nothing's true. I have to make truth of the situation.

How did I do it in my life? I picked certain people to be with and be around. They were the kind of people that were up front, as close to being up front as they could get. People that said what they meant. People that acted on what they said.

Danny created for himself an alternate reality which consisted of rules that would allow him to avoid the guilt from Vietnam. It allowed him to justify the level of aggression he took on after Philippe's death. It allowed him to continue to "raise the stakes" in his violence and it allowed him to see himself as a good person while he was doing it. However, it was superficial, and this reality required constant reinforcement in order for it to not come crashing in on him. It was that he needed to believe it in order to justify the anger that he had for himself as well as for society. Either society was right or he was right and he couldn't live with the possibility that he was wrong.

It seemed clear that Danny had deep emotional problems he was unable to live with. At one time he said had he gotten into therapy when he first got home that his postwar life would have been different. Instead, Danny was creating his own reality.

I started with an attitude that I didn't give a damn if any other people existed at all. I didn't think they were worth anything. So, I congregated with people who felt the same way. We isolated ourselves from the majority of people by being bikers. Who gets along with the bikers? Nobody but other bikers. That's the situation. We were racists, we were into drugs, we were into anything that was profitable. We didn't look at life with a conscience. We didn't ask ourselves if it would be bad for somebody else down the road. We really didn't give a damn. We moved into an "us and them" philosophy on everything.

The hate Danny had for others was a mirror image of the deep hate he had for himself. If a person feels angry there is the possibility of having times when he doesn't feel anger. However, if a person is anger it leaves no room for anything else. It's like being deep underground in a cave. There is no possibility of natural light and, in Danny's case, he would not consider the option of bringing in some light. He felt he was rejected by society so he opted to create his own reality which included only him and his other friends who believed as he did.

Did you have rules or some kind of code that you followed?

I've always had a code. Even when I looked around me and I saw that the rest of world don't adhere to my code. They pay lip service to my code but they don't follow it.
My code is the code. It goes all the way back to John Wayne and all our Sunday heroes. They all had the same code and I adopted theirs. It was all the way down inside of me. I was really loyal to my friends. I was courageous. The people I loved I loved completely with no reservations. Those were the things that I lived for.

His reality was governed by a code of ethics which placed him above everyone else. He was again making his point that everybody outside of his world was phony.

Now I had to find something to codify this code with the beliefs I started to have as a child. I had the same one in Vietnam and after I got home. I picked the Samurai, the code of Bushido. It exemplified my life as I saw me, as a warrior.

The code is not for material profiting. A man is a warrior and that's what a man should be. I had put myself in Vietnam and after Vietnam I'd put myself in war-type situations with us fighting with other biker clubs all over the country. It was still war and, as I said before, it's the only one we had. So, I adopted this code. It fit me at the time.

You seem to be talking about the past. Is it still your code or did you give it up?

It was my code and it still is. Even now, a lot of the things are the same. Loyalty, honesty, courage; those things are all part of Bushido. They are things the Samurai had. If I am going to give my sword, for instance, or my gun to somebody, I'm going to give it all the way, you know?

Now it could be heredity thing. If I was born into it, I would do it. Or if it is my own decision, then it's going to be for someone that I think is worthy, then I would go ahead and do it.

I asked Danny what he meant by being "born into it." He said the code of the Samurai had always felt natural to him. When he read about it as a child, it was not as if he was learning something for the first time, it was something already in him, something dormant, being awakened. He said it had always been something secret with him, something he didn't tell anyone except a few of his closest friends. He believed strongly that he had been a Samurai Warrior in a former life.

Later on, when I was in the bike club, I honestly did feel that the brothers of mine in the bike club were worthy. At one time I honestly felt that we were fighting for our freedom and our honor and to be able to be any way we decided to be. We didn't want nobody telling us it is going to be like this or it's going to be like that or anything else. Those kinds of things appeal to me. I don't care what the odds are and I have never been an odds man, you know. Except when the war was on and I had to figure what the odds were compared to what the enemy's strength was to ours in any given situation.

The Samurai code, the code of Bushido, is also that you make your own decisions. Nobody else is responsible for anything that you do but you. You are responsible. You have to make a decision in your head that something is right and then go ahead and do it. You make the decision in your head and if your heart tells you it's right, you act upon it. To not act upon it is a betrayal of yourself. The code kind of takes away all the nagging doubts of whether or not this is right or this is wrong.

As indicated previously, Danny was speaking of his version of the Samurai, and it worked temporarily. He never said that any others in his club were Samurai nor did the club view themselves as Samurai. His identification as a Samurai Warrior was a justification for his actions. His decision to kill the six NVA in Vietnam was later felt to be justified since if you didn't act on what your heart told you was right then it was a betrayal of yourself. And it was a betrayal of the code.

Were you always satisfied with your decisions?

For the most part, yes. I've met people who were thrill fighters and thrill killers, if you know what I mean. They do it all for the thrill of it. You see a whole hell of a lot of thrill fighters, guys who start fights all over the place. Even when they're in a situation where they can't win they'll start to fight because it's not about winning or losing, it's about the thrill of it going down.

But we've talked before about killing people. Something really profound is happening here. I don't think that anybody that's ever killed anyone will tell you that there's not something there that's nowhere else. I've never come across any other kind of activity that's anything like that. I didn't kill anyone unless I believed there was a good reason to do so.

Is there a relationship between bonding in the club and the bonding between you and members of your squad in Vietnam?

Yeah, exactly, it's exactly the same. To stand in the face of danger wasn't quite the same. It was a lot stronger in Vietnam but danger bonds men. It creates a specialness between you and them. I'll tell you something else that bikers do. If me and some of my friends are out on the street and you walk fairly close to me and I push you away, you may get angry and say something. Maybe I'll throw a couple of punches. Then all five or six of these guys with me will jump on you. It's not that they think I can't handle the situation, it's that no matter what happens all the guys are going to be part of it. It's just that way.

Which means the group had to have been functioning for at least some period of time, enough to build up that bonding.

> Yeah. Well, it's a constant. We would come up with things to create a bond. You remember what I said earlier about evil begets evil? We had a club of 100 or 150 members at any given time. You have to do something to keep you together. You have to have some reason to exist and you have to have some way to make the close connections.
>
> Part of it was fighting other people so you set up a situation that's basically evil in the first place.

What do you mean evil?

> I'm making the decisions on how I want to live and screw what you want. We had these patches that had FTW. It means F____ The World. Coming from that kind of attitude is basically evil anyway. So, you've got to perpetuate that attitude to keep yourselves together and to maintain the bond. The feeling was us against them whether it was made verbal or not.

Danny's behavior and attitudes were sanctioned by the other members of the club and, in particular, his close friends who had also served with in Vietnam. He became the head of security in the club, allowing him to maintain many of the same policies and tactics in the club activities as had worked for him in Vietnam.

His distorted interpretation of the Samurai Code allowed him to feel justified in his criminal activities in spite of believing himself to be a reincarnated Samurai Warrior bound by honor, justice, and loyalty. It's extremely difficult to have an image in your mind as a child of wanting to be a Sir Lancelot or King Arthur and later having an identity of being evil and of choosing to live in the dark. The fact he insisted that living in the dark was a complete life suggests that he wouldn't allow himself to consider alternative ways to live. Danny had his concept of reality and he molded his environment and the people in it to fit that reality.

A firm rule in his code was that he would never harm women, children, or old people because they were innocent.

FOURTEEN

Danny and Charlie

When Danny's friend, Philippe, got killed in Vietnam, Danny experienced a dramatic change in his personality. It began with dissociation. Everything became dreamlike and he lost the capacity to experience fear. Danny felt he was no longer a foreigner in a strange country and felt natural in his surroundings. He said he was never afraid of anything after that. He took dangerous chances where he could easily have been killed. This transformation changed him from a Marine on the line shooting at the enemy into a dynamic leader who aggressively went after them. The change appears to have become permanent.

At one time I had another client who had been in Vietnam. He along with other soldiers was transported by helicopter into an area that had been reported by military intelligence to be "clean." That is, the area had been scouted out and no enemy forces had been detected. The military objective was to drop these troops into the enemy-free area and from there they would move towards another area where the enemy was known to be.

While he and others were parachuting down into the field they suddenly came under fire. Enemy soldiers were all around them and he watched helplessly as his friends were shot while still in the air. He landed, quickly exited from his chute, and ran to a small area of brush for protection. He said he pressed as close to the ground as he could get because the enemy saw him go in where there was minimal protection against bullets.

He was terrified and anticipated being hit by a bullet at any moment. He felt a sudden change come over him and he was no longer afraid. He grabbed his rifle, stood up, and began firing and running towards a clump of trees where he thought the enemy fire was coming from. He reached the trees, killed three Vietcong, and was later given a medal for his heroism. He said he didn't do it out of desperation, but that another personality was created when he was behind the brush. Unfortunately, this was not a temporary change. He continued to have this other personality for years after that. Danny may have experienced something similar to what this other soldier experienced but perhaps to a lesser degree. I never saw anything in Danny which would suggest a Dissociative Identity Disorder. However, maybe Danny had something similar to it.

Did you ever feel that you were more than one person? That is, when you would go into a fight did you ever feel that you were in some kind of an altered state? Did it ever seem like it was not you doing the fighting but someone or something else?

Did I ever think I was more than one person? Yeah, I have had that. I used to think that, and I still do to a degree, but it's less now. I always felt like there was more than one person here. I used to argue with myself in my head. It didn't seem natural that a person would have in their mind two people who have absolutely opposite points of view on something, but that's how it was with me. I have had trouble with that all of my life. I used to argue both sides of every issue.

Even before Vietnam?

Not so much before then, I can't really say if that is true or not.

Is it like something inside of you is arguing against you?

Yeah, it seems like somebody ... not necessarily arguing, but pointing out all of the pitfalls. I didn't know if that was just me. A lot of times I would get really mad at myself for that.

Would you ever be surprised about what this other part was saying?

Not really. I was always aware of what this other side was bringing up. It seemed like I had a thing, like another person, in me, another type. Kate can remember me telling her about wanting to go into the police station. That was a fantasy I had a lot. You know, I was thinking about going on T.V. and telling them about how screwed up the world is and everything. I wanted to make this point and I figured they would listen if I blew away half of the police force. They might listen then and I would tell them how terrible the world is and how crappy they are as human beings. Then I would kill myself in the end.

But getting back to the thing we were talking about. I remember I used to consider myself as more than one person for sure. I used to think of myself as Charlie. Charlie was mean. When something would come up Charlie would be in control. He was absolutely calculating all of the way down the line, absolutely vicious. That was Charlie.

Did you always remember everything Charlie did?

Yeah, everything. It wasn't like we were separate or that there was another personality. It wasn't anything like that. I always considered I had, not another person, but something that would come over me any time that I was about to be really violent. That could be a fight or just getting ready to be violent. That was Charlie. Charlie always won because Charlie was going to win.

Remember how I told you the other side of me would argue about what could happen? I was very indecisive. I mean it could go on and on and on and just drive you right up the wall. Charlie would have none of that. Charlie would make a decision and he would have absolute focus.

Was there any indecision when you would be in that Charlie state and would do whatever he was going to do?

> Charlie would take no advice from nobody. Charlie knew the situation and he always made the right choices. He didn't mess with nothing and actually Charlie was contemptuous of the choices. You know the people who sit around and think well, well, will paralyze themselves with the possibilities. Charlie was action. Charlie was violence.

When Charlie was doing what Charlie was doing did you feel like you were in control? Some people say it was as if they were watching or it was happening to them. How would you experience it?

> I never thought of it that way before. This was the first time I've ever heard it put like that. I think I felt like it was Charlie and it wasn't me.
>
> Charlie was on automatic. It was almost like I was watching it but it was like I had seen it before. Maybe this is where the calmness came in because I had absolute belief in Charlie. Charlie didn't have any fear. He was absolutely sure of himself in what he was going to do and how he was going to do it.
>
> Charlie would do whatever he had to do and he didn't worry about anything. That combination of ingredients is hard to beat. I had absolute confidence in that persona. It would work every time. I don't know if I thought that out or how I ever came to that but it was like I felt absolutely calm because he was in charge and he was going to do it right.

. . .

Did you ever feel like you wanted to stop what Charlie was doing?

Never. Not until I got into therapy.

When Charlie would come on and start doing whatever he was going to do, did you feel it was Charlie and not you?

I felt like I was doing it too. It was Charlie and me. I never had a thought that this was somebody else and that I didn't know what was going on. This was me, but it was how I wanted to be.

I wanted to be like Charlie. Charlie had no problems. He had everything under control and he would do whatever he had to do in any situation. A lot of times I was paralyzed by doubts. Not about what I was doing in a situation but it was about what I should do. I couldn't make a decision. There would be times when I would be sitting around the house thinking I should go do this or that but I couldn't make up my mind.

Then I would get frustrated and I would start to get angry and Charlie would set it all right.

What would be the final trigger that would cause you to make the shift into that Charlie state?

Usually it was anger. But if we were coming up on something that we were going to do, Charlie would be in control the whole way. That was Charlie the whole way. That was Charlie before we got there. That was Charlie going through everything. That was all Charlie because that was Charlie's thing.

What would you feel when that happened?

I would feel good because I wasn't fighting with myself. I would feel absolutely calm and it would be like boom, boom, boom, boom, set them up and knock them down.

And you would function all right?

I would function absolutely great. Most people knew me as Charlie. They didn't know that it was another side of me, but when they would think of me they would think of me as Charlie.

One time you said that when you were in a supermarket you thought about killing some of the people there. Was that you or Charlie?

That would be me, but it depends if I was in Charlie at the time. I could make up that scenario and stuff but the trouble with that is that if it was me I would also think that there might be a chance that something could go wrong. I would argue with myself over that. I wasn't looking for trouble but Charlie was and that was the difference between us.

Did I tell you about the story of the guy I drew down on in a swap meet? That was Charlie. Did I tell you that story?

No, I don't remember that you did. What happened?

There was this one particular guy that I thought was an absolute waste of time. I didn't want to specifically kill that guy, but I would have. He was an absolute waste of space and he was an absolute waste of a human being. He was a mean, dirty, nasty dude that demeaned people on a constant basis. I mean he was one of those that was wild in the eyes and always was looking to mess with somebody. And it ran the gambit from beating people up through talking bad about them. He was just that kind of individual.

Now, we had only had a couple of times when we had dealings with each other. One of them was when me and someone from our club went down to speak to them about something and we were trying to get them to come over to us in the beginning, and this is where this started with this guy. I actually wanted to kill him that time but that was not the time or the place or the situation to do it.

It was just the way he ran his mouth. All I could do then was argue with this guy and the last thing in the world I wanted to do was to talk to this idiot. He didn't want to argue to make a point. He wanted to argue to show off and put me and the other guys in our club down. We couldn't do anything about it at the time but I never forgot this guy.

We completed our transactions with him and his group and we left. Well, I ran into him a few years later and he's acting like now we're long lost friends and stuff and I still can't stand him.

We were at a swap meet. I tried to ignore him as much as possible but he grated on me. He was still running his mouth like he was a mean dude and was better than everybody else. I wanted to humiliate him and make him back up what he was pretending to be. I wanted to put him in the situation that I had seen him put so many other people in, even me and my people. He tried to humiliate us but he couldn't do it.

The deal was that we were supposed to be unarmed at that meet, but some of us were carrying just in case. I remember I was standing there and we were all shooting the shit. He said something and I said something back and then he said something back, you know what I'm talking about? It was escalating so I walked about 6 to 8 feet away, maybe 10 feet away, and there were people all around. He was sitting down and I was standing up and I walked away. And I had a real long leather coat on. I threw my coat back and I had my pistol stuck in my belt and I said, "Draw! Go for it!"

He looked at me and everybody first thought like this was really funny. I kept staring at him and I said, "Go for your gun or I am going to kill you!" He had a gun but he didn't go for it. He said back, "I don't want any trouble with you." Then everybody started to freak. They all told me not to do it. I said, "I'm going to kill you if you don't go for it." My friends all got in between me and him and then he just wimped out. I said to him, "Come on if you're such a bad ass, you're such a killer. Come on and show me because I am going to kill you if you don't! If you don't go for that gun, I am going to kill you anyway."

He had pretended that he was such a mean ass but when I challenged him he had nowhere to go and hide. He had to come out and say, "I'm not a real killer." He actually didn't say it but that is what he was screaming loud about because he wouldn't fight. He wouldn't go for his gun and I wouldn't give him any peace. I kept hollering at him even as he was trying to leave and my friends were trying to keep me from shooting the heck out of him. They were coming out in front of me and stuff so I couldn't pull my pistol out and shoot him. They figured I would. You know, I just did stuff like that. I mean Charlie would do things like that.

I remember when me and this other dude went into a bar where only blacks were allowed. We went on in, sat down, and asked for a drink. They all looked at us and the bartender didn't want to give it to us. We were like, "You're going to give us the drink." He gave us the drinks. Someone said, "Why don't you get the hell out of here!" I said, "Why don't you throw us out!" They didn't. They looked at us and said, "No, you guys are nuts." I did a lot of stuff like that.

When you would have a fantasy, say, when you were by yourself and had time to have a fantasy, how real would it be?

It would be really real. It would be so real sometimes that I would hold my breath through it and didn't even know it. I would catch my breath afterwards. Sometimes it would be amazingly real. A lot of times maybe different ladies would be around and they would wonder what was happening.

What would they be seeing in you?

I didn't want to talk about it. I didn't want to get into it because if they asked me about it I didn't want to tell them. They would be thinking I was thinking of some other woman.

Would it ever seem like you were watching it on a screen?

I suppose it was always that way. It was like I was watching it in a movie or on the television or something, and I would see it all go down. I would run a quick scenario about who, what, why, when, and where. I would make it up as I went along, usually, or make it up really fast about this person did that and I did that and I would have to go here and I had seen him here and he was going to be here, bingo. It would take a couple of minutes. It would all be over in two to three minutes.

How would you feel afterwards?

I would always feel pepped up somehow by it, lifted up. You know, it's a funny thing. I could be on an expressway or something and some guy would shoot past me. I may think about following him off the expressway somewhere, catching him when he gets out of his car, and then, poom. And I would still be driving while I was thinking about all this.

Would you ever get a feeling of peace after one of these fantasies in comparison to the real thing?

Not like that. If anything, it was phony. Momentary at best. But I used to have a million of these. A million of them.

FIFTEEN

Escalating to Murder

Although Danny was heavily involved with the operations of the club, it wasn't enough. He and other leaders gave orders for crimes to be committed and members of the club carried out their orders. It was an efficient procedure since Danny could supervise the action to make sure it was done right. The tasks were completed successfully, but this wasn't enough for him. He wanted to be more directly involved.

He had said that he felt a need to keep raising the stakes until it came to murder. He had always considered himself to be a soldier rather than a leader. As in Vietnam, he wanted to be personally involved in the elimination of an enemy, not just giving orders to have it done. As head of security for the club, he had the authority to do it.

The time came when some people who were enemies of the club needed to be dealt with through more than threats and intimidation. Danny, in his need to keep raising the stakes, said he wanted to take care of it. He would eliminate the enemy. However, "My friends didn't want me to do this.

We had other people who could do it." Some of these friends were hit men. Danny said,

> I know a few guys that contract now. They contracted then and they contract now. Each and every one of them is smarter than the average individual. They really are. None of them are stupid or plodding. Hit men are not physically oriented people. They are intelligent. You can get an amateur to kill somebody for $50.00. The professional is different. They may live together but they are loners. They are good at many things and they are well read and they often like activities such as chess.
>
> I remember the first time. I said no, I'll go down and I'll take care of it. We had a big discussion about it. I said, "No, this has to be done and I can do it best, you know. I'll take care of it." It was actually okay if one of the others did it, but each and every time it was like that was my job. I was head of security. That was my job. I could have had a lot of people to do this for me but I needed to do it.

Was there no other way you could handle the situation than to kill him?

> What they were doing was like a gangrene spot in the arm. I wasn't about to operate on the gangrene and try to get it off. I cut the arm off. I could have put forth an argument of whether we can teach this guy a lesson, but I didn't believe the guy should be taught a lesson! I really didn't care what the person was doing as long as it was detrimental to us in any shape, form, or another. That's it. I didn't care why he done it, I didn't care about a lesson being taught

here. I wanted the whole arm off. Then you're through with the problem. You don't ever have to worry about that gangrenous spot coming back. You don't have to worry if you got it all or not.

There would come a point in the conversation when Danny would shift into the mindset of Charlie and there would be a change in his personality. While Danny would stumble around indecisively in a conversation, Charlie wouldn't. Danny's girlfriend said that when he got angry he looked like a different person.

As I've indicated earlier, Danny was not a split personality. Danny always knew what Charlie was doing. Charlie was fearless—on automatic pilot—and focused sharply on the main issue with absolute confidence. The Charlie state wouldn't do anything that Danny didn't want to do. In Nam, when in the firefights, everybody would become terrified but Danny would get calm. This was Charlie.

Danny had this to a degree when he was a teenager. He was on the school football team and prior to a game he would be physically sick, but as soon as the first hit came on the field, the anxiety left him.

Why was it so necessary for you to do that first hit?

Everything in life is boring. That is the problem with being good. Nam is very exciting and nothing ever reaches that level of excitement. After you have killed somebody in Nam, nothing else is as exciting. Killing is an addiction.

In what way?

> When I killed somebody, I felt fine. Actually, I was high. It's like being addicted to coke. The urge comes on stronger when you are bored or depressed. Neither drugs nor alcohol would work. Only killing would bring me to where I wanted to be, to feel human and feel natural emotions. Otherwise I was emotionally dead.

Earlier when we talked about how you changed when Philippe was killed, you said that you had lost your capability to feel emotions other than anger and depression. You hadn't yet killed anyone since the war but now you were voluntarily about to kill again. Why?

> There's a permanence to death. When you kill someone, you can't take it back. There is an unreality to it.

Has the thought of your own death ever bothered you?

> I think I have always thought more of how I would die than dying itself. I have never been bothered of the fact that I was going to die, even when I was really young and they were trying to force Christianity on me. I will give you an example that might shine some light on it. I remember when I was a small boy, I must have been ten, and I saw this movie about American prisoners of war during World War II. The Japanese had these prisoners and they were feeding them kernels of corn in the snow. This one guy's friend was sick so he stole some medicine

from the Japs to help his friend. The Japs caught him and they tied him up and put his feet in a pan of water. He died right away.

I remember going to bed right after that was over and got under the covers and was crying. I was thinking, don't let this happen to me. Don't let this happen this way. It wasn't about that I would die from this, but I might break from this. If they did me like this, they might break me somehow. I have always been more frightened of how I die than dying itself.

Were you ever afraid that you could get killed in a contract operation?

No. I believed that if I was careful and planned it out that nothing would happen to me.

Take me through the process. You're with your friends and someone brings up the issue about an enemy you are having problems with. What is going through your mind while the conversation is taking place?

When we talked about doing a hit I would take the lead in order to control the conversation.

Why was that necessary?

I knew where the conversation was going and I wanted to make my point first. It's easier to control a conversation from the beginning than to try to change it in the middle.

Okay, go on. I'm interested in what you were thinking during the conversation.

My thoughts would start out more as if in slow motion and they would rush more at the end. When the conversation would get to where the city was of the person who was to be eliminated my thinking would start to become more dream-like.

I would take the hit man role in the conversation. I would become that person in my mind. I would actually feel like I was him. I would feel absolutely perfect in it. That's where the kick comes from. I am that person and everything is right. You feel all confident and all the other insecurities are gone.

Would you consider the possibility of something going wrong?

If something goes wrong all you have to do is to think what you were going to do. You have every right to be that way. You live the role, and you're perfect for it. I firmly believe anybody can do it. We all have our ideas of what a hit man is. I don't like admitting it, but it's true. There were times when I wanted to speak out against what we were doing but I needed to do it.

. . .

You mean there were times when you weren't sure whether or not you wanted to kill the guy? If so, why did you decide to go ahead with it?

Violence is a funny thing. You are either for it or against it. You can't be neutral. Your body reacts to it, either for or against it. Violence almost has a life of its own.

There was violence in our group of bikers. There was a constant urge towards violence under the surface and anything could touch it off. It was necessary for us to act it out. It was as if we were all kind of waiting for something to happen that would allow us to be violent. Remember I told you that we would bop the boulevard? We would go downtown where the pimps and chicks were. We would walk down the sidewalk and take it all up and people would have to walk around us.

Yeah, I remember you talking about that. What would it do for you?

There was a tremendous feeling of power. Everybody feeds off it and it feeds off us. It has a life all its own. It's really relaxing after it's over. It builds up then it's relaxing.

There's a heightened sense of control, absolute control. It's a dead feeling. You feel that it's impossible to make a mistake. It's so close to what you have visualized like it's locked in to happen that way. In Nam the bullets went to just where I wanted them to go. You only have one opportunity to hurt the enemy before he hurts you. A person who is not into violence can't understand that. I never thought that I didn't want to hurt him too bad.

When you got that urge that you want to go out and destroy something or someone, did that change your view of reality? What are your thoughts on that?

First off, you have to be convinced that you have the absolute right to do what you're doing. And I believe beyond a doubt every one of these guys, every person that does a hit, has that. In order to kill somebody on contract you have to have that. You have to believe that you have the absolute right to do what you are doing. Now for me ... I can only speak for me on this. It had a real calming effect on me. You know, this is a hell of thing to say, but the truth of it is it gave me more peace than I had at any other time.

That was after the event?

Yeah, well, it was even building up to the event. There was a ritual to it.

As you got into the ritual then it was calm from then on?

Well it seems like I had something in me that sort of triggered the calmness when I knew I had to do this ... that I was going to do this. You notice how I said I had to do it? I don't think I could have not done it.

When I knew I was going to do it, it would trigger the thought that I had a right to do it. Then everything would be slowed down and put more into perspective and it's like I would exercise more control over everything. Controlling every aspect of everything that went down. Everything that had to happen and for those periods of time I would visualize how things would go.

Would this just be in the planning of it or would you be more controlling in everything you did throughout the day?

I didn't do that on like an everyday basis in other things that happened in my life, I really didn't. But in these specific instances I would visualize what's going to happen and how it's going to happen. I'm talking about getting a transfer of vehicles to getting the weapon to getting everything down. I'm talking of how the other people involved with it are going to react. I'm not talking about the person who gets killed, I'm talking about the people that were involved in supplying arms. I would visualize that I'm going to leave at such and such time and arrive at a place at such and such time, right? I would visualize the trip before I left.

You wouldn't feel it though?

No. I wouldn't feel it or anything. I would just visualize how the trip's going to go. We're not talking about a long, drawn-out process, just a quick look ahead at what it's about. Okay, then when I would get there or get close to getting there I would visualize the situation of what's happening next. Who I'm going to see—these types of situations. It's really odd for those people involved. They did not know what was happening. They just knew what they had been told to do by someone else, that's all they knew.

They knew something bad was going to go down, something criminal was going to go down. They were in the criminal light so they knew something was going to go down but they didn't have any idea what. Maybe they were going to supply a vehicle or maybe a place for me to stay a few days. Maybe a weapon or maybe all three, you know. I would only have contact with one or maybe two people tops, that's it. And they had no idea what I was doing down there or who I was. Names were never used.

I would envision the way it was to go down. If something would not go the way I had envisioned it to go, then I would make it go that way.

What do you mean?

I would get angry and I would come across to these people like this is how this goes.

Would your contacts ever back out?

Not if they wanted to remain friends with us.

Was there a common element about the people you wanted to eliminate?

That's an interesting question. I hadn't considered that. If you want to look at it and put it in some context, each one of these people that I personally dealt with had betrayed us one way or the other. That was a common denominator. They had either betrayed us by breaking their commitment to us in the middle of a biker war or they had betrayed us by trying to rip something off from us while we were occupied with the war. Some were trying to rip us off in our drug business. Then there were some people who were just in the way, people that didn't do one thing one way or the other.

Do your friends who are also hit men have rituals or patterns as to how they carry out a contract?

Yeah, they follow a pattern because they understand it and they feel more comfortable with it. They probably felt like I felt. It's more preparation than anything else. What I did was positive imagery. You know what I'm talking about? When you visualize a situation and go through it in your mind's eye as to exactly how it's supposed to go down, then it usually goes down exactly that way.

How often would you go through that imagery?

You know something? Probably the day I was getting ready to do that it was almost a constant thing. I'd go through it then I'd go through it again and I'd go through this part of it and I'd go through that part of it and I'd go through this other part of it. It was almost a constant thing.

And you know something? It's not only of those situations though. I've done that with a lot of things in my life. I have a deep belief in that. I didn't know that was positive imagery until later on, but I've always believed you have to envision doing it the way it's supposed to be done. I used to do that when I was in football games and in wrestling. I'd visualize just what I was going to do. I believed superstitiously that if you did not do that then it wouldn't come down that way.

Why do you think you had so much distrust? Was there anybody you believed in?

You know something? In my entire life I've never had any heroes other than some guys I knew on the streets. Even now, I don't have any heroes. Period. I believe that everybody will let you down sooner or later. I think very little of most people, period. That's a direct result of Nam. The guys I killed I thought they had absolutely nothing coming. They were worse than ... if you just let it alone was not good enough. You know what I'm talking about? Because they would turn on you in a heartbeat.

What about Nam changed your mind? You didn't seem to feel this way before you went there.

No, I didn't. I don't know. Nam was such a serious business. As a squad leader I had to keep close track of my men.

You know what I did one night? I had these guys out at a forward listening post. It was raining. It was during the monsoon. What happened was I was standing lines with my squad. Most squad leaders they got to sleep all night but they had to get up and check their lines three times during the night. My guys at the listening post were to call in and give a SR [situation report] to the lieutenant at the command post every 15 minutes. If they didn't report in, the command post would call them. If you're secure all you do is key the handset twice. If it's not secure you key it once. You know what I mean? You never speak because you've got to be quiet.

The command post got no response from my listening post. They were out in front of me about 50 to 75 yards, a little bit into the jungle. Someone came down and said, "Hey, you're listening post is not answering." I didn't think about the possibility that anything might have happened to them. You know what I thought? They went to sleep! I grabbed my rifle and took off out there. I didn't think about my safety. It was raining. Here they were, all three of them asleep. I started kicking them, stomping them. It was crazy as hell when you think about it. [Laughs]. I was so mad. They all pointed fingers at each other as to who was supposed to be on watch. [Laughs] I kicked the hell out of them.

It was a crazy episode. I was so mad. I couldn't believe they would crawl out there in the weeds and go to sleep. Are you kidding me? It didn't make any sense to me all. I could never understand that. What the hell! Why didn't you just go boom [gun firing]? Then you could sleep for all eternity if that's what you need!

We had guys falling asleep but not in my squad! In

other squads guys would fall asleep all the time. I couldn't get a grip on that. I really could never understand it and I would not allow it. Not only is a guy risking his life by falling asleep, he's risking the lives of the other two guys with him. Not only that, he's risking our lives too. The enemy can get closer to us when we think we're secure. If something happens out there, they can't let us know. It's risking everybody's life.

It never crossed my mind that these guys would sleep out on watch. I marched down there really mad. I was really pissed off and there lay all three of them. I started stomping on them and they were hollering. It was a weird thing. It was really strange.

SIXTEEN

The First Hit

T he time came for his first contract. The arrangements
were made and Danny left to go to the city where the
hit was to take place. He arrived three days prior to the
scheduled time. His purpose of arriving that early was to be
able to check the accuracy of the information he had been
given. He stayed in a motel under a false name. He watched
the victim at various times during the day and into the night
until the man retired for the night and shut off all the lights
in his home. The victim had previously been scouted out and
Danny had an agenda of the person's movements. Danny
knew who was in the home, he knew when the victim would
first arrive home, and he knew if the guy had meetings or
other activities scheduled and the nights when they were to
occur.

On the morning of the planned event, Danny showered,
had a light breakfast and then took his weapon apart and
cleaned each piece and put it back together again. He took a
small amount of heroin, which he did every day, and
watched TV. He had three beers throughout the day and
when the appointed time came he traveled across the city to

where the action was to take place. He had a stolen license plate on his cycle and the gun he was using had also been stolen. He wore gloves so he wouldn't leave any prints. He obeyed all the traffic laws to minimize the chance that he would stand out in any way. It was fairly late at night when most people were already off the streets and in their homes. The time and place of the hit had been carefully planned.

His original plan was to meet the guy face to face. However, the guy was carrying a sack of garbage out to the dumpster. Danny was standing behind a wall in the dark and when the man walked past him, Danny stepped out behind the guy and said "boo." He shot him twice, first in the head and then in the heart.

> I turned away and walked back through—it was a darkened garage, carport thing, whatever you want to call it, where the people in the apartment building park their cars because there was no other place to park them. I walked through it and it was dark down at the other end and I just walked through all the way down to the other end and, as I was walking, I dropped the weapon, pulled the gloves off, walked over, got on my motorcycle, and shot down the road. I took about two or three turns, threw the gloves away, and kept driving. There was nothing to it. I mean I felt absolutely calm. I wasn't afraid. I didn't feel that I had done anything wrong at all. I did not feel that. I have to say that.

He rode across town to the safe house where he remained until it was safe to leave the city. The people in the safe house weren't aware that he had been in town for the past few days and they were not aware of the homicide. When the homicide hit the news, no questions were asked.

How did it affect you?

> It was profound. Right off the bat. Immediately. This sounds really phony but I think I was even going through it before it actually happened because I was so familiar with death anyway. Death was something I had never been able to shake from Nam. It lived with me. The act itself of taking somebody else's life. It lived in me. It lived with me the whole time, in Nam and when I came home. As this guy came walking up to me I knew he was dead. You know what I mean? While he was still alive. I felt really calm about the whole thing because I had seen so much death and I had done it before. As he was coming towards me I could see he had no weapon, and if he did have one hid on him somewhere he couldn't get to it in time. So that whole thing was like it was already finished. It was already done.

You said earlier that you are never more alive than when you are in the face of death. Did you feel that sense of being alive when you shot him?

> Absolutely. And every other time as well, Nam included, and the events I was involved afterwards, there was never a time when I didn't feel it at that time, right before, right during, and right after, and for a length of time after that. I felt that I was practically omnipotent. You know what I mean? God-like. Because your senses ... I felt ... almost

felt out of body in a sense but it wasn't like I was looking at it. You know what I mean?

But I had ... had a ... a feeling, like everything is working on automatic or something. You know what I mean? It's like I don't specifically have to think about anything. Everything was previously thought of. It's a ... it's a ... I felt nothing is going to go wrong. Everything was going to go the way it was supposed to go. I was doing this absolutely the way it was supposed be done and I was absolutely right about the whole situation. Not only that but it's like all your senses are sharpened. Your hearing is really attuned. It's like I didn't think for a moment that I could be taken by surprise. I wasn't fearful of anything.

You had no fear of getting caught?

It's very easy to kill somebody on a contract and you are not likely to get caught. The only way you are going to get caught is if the cops bump into you on the spot because you're not from there, you have no motive tying you to this individual, unless you look like the road warrior or something strange.... Look at me, how are you going to describe me? A witness is going to describe me as, "Well he's approximately 5' 8", brown hair, brown eyes, 150 lbs." That fits about half of the guys in the world. And I'm not from there and I'll soon be gone from there.

Did it seem to satisfy something in you?

It took care of something. It did something. I wish I could be more specific on exactly what it did do for me but it brought me a sense of peace for a while. Something profound is happening right here, right now when that goes down. I imagine if somebody was in control of almost of all of their emotions and wasn't emotionally dead like I was, or emotionally numb, it would've been a really exhilarating experience.

I knew he was dead, you know. It wasn't like I thought he might not be dead. I mean he was through. I felt absolutely nothing, I mean I felt absolutely calm about the whole thing and it was a matter of going through the things I had already set out and rehearsed doing in my head.

Were you able to take responsibility for the person's death?

I didn't believe I was responsible for his death. I killed him but he was responsible for his death.

What do you mean? Can you for a moment separate the act of killing from responsibility for death?

This is going to sound weird, but I didn't connect the two, that I was killing someone and they were dying. I knew for a fact that I was killing them and they would be dead, but I didn't put it together that I was killing you, therefore you are dead. You know, that connection. That is strange because up until you said that in those terms it was exactly what I did.

It's hard for me to make the connection because I thought in terms of these guys were trying to hurt us. I knew what they were trying to do to us wouldn't kill us, but you have to stop it somewhere and you can't let anybody steal from you and push you around. Especially at the time you have to take everything into consideration of what was going on. We were struggling to hold what we had together. We were close and believed in each other and believed in what we were doing.

I knew I was killing those people and all that says, except that somehow I wasn't responsible for their death. I did kill them, but I wasn't responsible for their death. They were responsible for their deaths so there was a difference. I thought if they hadn't done what they did to us and were trying to do to us, they wouldn't be dead and I wouldn't have killed them. You might say that is some kind of back-handed justification, but the facts are that I didn't think of them as dead from me. I knew for a fact I killed them, if you can make that connection. I didn't feel that I was causing their death even though I knew beyond a shadow of a doubt I was killing them. That was what I was there for.

About how long was it between then and the second one?

It was about eight months later.

Between then were there any nightmares, did you think about the guy?

I thought about him from time to time but I didn't feel remorse for his death. I had thoroughly convinced myself, and still believe to this day, we were all soldiers in this thing. He was a soldier too just like I was. These people were in this game and they would kill, too. It's not like they were innocent. I wouldn't kill anybody that wasn't somehow connected to us or the cocaine trade one way or another.

Following this homicide, Danny went back to the club and returned to his normal routine. He had a feeling of peace as well as feeling satisfied.

I felt it right afterwards. It lasted a long time and even drugs didn't dull that feeling because I immediately went and did some dope as soon as I could. I got back to where I was staying and I shot some heroin. It really didn't dull the feeling. It was almost like a cocaine-heroin mixture high, a really nice high. An intense but mellow high. Those are contradictory terms but it's true. It's the same kind of feeling. That's as close as I can come to … it's not the same exactly but it's close. That kind of high.

SEVENTEEN

The Second Hit

D anny was fighting a parallel war here at home that was similar to the war he had fought in Vietnam. Over there he was fighting the NVA. Here at home he was fighting drug dealers. In Vietnam, he took the fight to the enemy whenever he could with such things as going point on patrols and going out beyond the lines at night where he would sit in the grass and wait for an NVA to crawl up to him. In his contract homicides he again took it to the enemy.

Both operations took planning, skill, and patience. In Vietnam he felt excitement when he was hunting the enemy and peace when he was able to conquer one of them. In the bike club he felt excitement when planning the hunt and during the elimination of the enemy. Afterwards he felt peace. In Vietnam he ascribed his need for revenge to the loss of Philippe and other friends. In the bike club he felt a need to eliminate people who brought harm to the members of his club. In Nam he felt a strong need to protect the troops in his squad, his family. Here at home, as the head of security, he had the same need to protect his family. In Nam when he killed the six enemy soldiers he was cutting off the gangrenous arm rather than saving or curing it. He was doing the same here.

In Vietnam no matter how many of the enemy he killed it wasn't enough. He never felt he was able to even up the score for what he felt the enemy had personally done to him. Even here at home he had a strong urge to finish the task he had set out to do when Philippe was killed.

Why did he have to keep raising the stakes towards murder here at home? And, once he had his first successful hit, why was he not able to say that it was enough? That he was done with killing? Why did he have to keep searching out the enemy and eliminating them? He didn't know it at the time but as with the six wounded enemy soldiers, no matter how many contracts he accepted, it would never be enough.

About eight months later he had the opportunity to do another hit.

> We had been trying to lure a large Detroit motorcycle gang into our camp and they were on the fence. I had been to Detroit twice to talk but we weren't getting very far along with this group. They tried to kill me. They shot up a car I was in and they shot my cousin who was in the car with me.

Why did they want to kill you?

- They were leaning more towards going with the Angels than us. And what happened is they shot the crap out of my cousin's car with me in it and they shot my cousin but they didn't get me. It didn't kill him.

- A few months later down the road things were going better between us and the Angels. The tide was starting to shift in our favor and this biker group was still on the fence. What happened was I set them up. I had gotten two guys to hit these dudes when they were coming to Chicago to negotiate. I had already put two guys on this to do this.

- The night before it went down I decided to join them. There was supposed to just be two guys from this bike club but there were three. Actually, there was more than that but there were three that we were going to be able to get our hands on at one time. We kidnapped these three and put them in a van and took them out in the sticks in the country. We were going to kill these guys.

This was different from the first hit.

It was not only different because we eliminated three of them, it was different because there were three of us doing it. It was also different because it was the only time I ever had an opportunity for any prolonged ... conversation with ... anybody that I knew I was going to kill. I had never had that length of time so ... I ended up taunting these guys about what we were going to do to them. It was really strange because ... this kid kept saying that we were only doing this because of his race. We took them out in this field and we all shot them. We all shot each one of them. Each of the three of us shot each one of them.

. . .

As you were taunting this kid on the way out of town, how did you feel inside? Psychologically, what were you going through?

> I was … I was … I was in great form, if you know what I mean. I was … talking. I was high, and I don't mean on drugs. I was up. For me it was personal because they had not only tried to kill me but they had shot my cousin. Not these particular guys. I don't know who, but I know it was from them. I was giving it back.

The similarity between this event and the six soldiers he executed in Vietnam is striking. He could not kill the person who shot at him and his cousin because he didn't know who it was, so he decided to kill others from that club. In Vietnam he was not able to get even by killing the person who killed Philippe so he executed six others in an attempt to satisfy his need to get even. As to what he thought or felt while taking these three guys out to the spot where they would eliminate them he said,

> It was more of a personal thing. I wasn't as detached as I usually was. I was really involved. But, then again, it could have been the length of time I spent with them. It could have been that too. I really don't know. But I was really up. Actually, I think I was more nervous … because it was different. I wasn't prepared … I was prepared but I hadn't experienced anything quite like this. We took them out in the field … actually it was a lot like the Nam one.

. . .

Was there a subconscious need to reenact the execution of the six NVA soldiers? Was it possible that maybe this time Danny would feel that it was finally over?

When you were out in the field were there any flashbacks of killing the six in Nam?

It wasn't like a flashback but it ... well, actually, I guess it was. It was like the similarities were obvious, you know. These guys were on their knees.

Did you have any feeling that you were in Nam at the time?

No. I felt like ... I think that for one of the first times ... though I have to say, there was something strange about this compared to what I did in Nam. At the time I really didn't feel like I executed those enemy soldiers in Nam. That was war and it was what went on in war. With this, though, I really started thinking about that maybe I had executed those soldiers in Nam. Until this time, I considered what I did in Nam was okay because of what they had done to Philippe. You know what I mean? They had got their hands on him. But it was like I was doing sort of the same thing.

So, it was similar.

Yeah, I was getting even for what they had done to us.

What did you feel right after you shot these guys and in the time period after that?

It was really different from the first one. The whole thing was different. I was with other guys on this one. After, we went back and got drunk and got high. Partied actually, and just kind of blended in where we were supposed to be, partying.

Any feeling of detachment when you traveled from the field back to the place where you had the party?

You know how I said I was anxious on the way out? All of that was gone. I was absolutely calm afterwards. I was into … whatever you want to call it … I was into this mood … peace, and I felt like I had won something.

Any idea what thoughts went through your mind on that trip back?

For the first time I started thinking of those guys in Nam and the similar situation. I was thinking about that when we were going back. And I was also thinking about these two guys who were with me.

What were you thinking about them?

I don't know. I had a tough time with that. It was my idea that everybody shoot everybody, so therefore we all do the same thing.

Why all of you shoot each rather than each one of you shooting one person?

I don't know. It seemed like to me that if we all did exactly the same thing then they would have to keep their mouths shut—although they could have turned state's evidence. I worried about them and you know something? I think they were worried about me, but they were worried about me in a different way. I don't think they were worried about me telling on them. I think they were worried that I might decide to clean the slate to make sure that nothing would ever be said about it.

When you came back and got drunk, was it just for the night?

In the situation we were in, we were drunk every day. It depended on what you had to do, you know. These guys were mine. They were secure. The guys I really kept tabs on. This was my responsibility. I knew everything about all of them, actually, and I mean everything. When they changed girlfriends, I knew it. We were like the Gestapo. Actually, there were a lot of those terms applied to us. The Nazi terminology. But just to the security portion of our outfit. I was head of security.

. . .

Danny was solidifying his position in the club as not only head of security but as a hit man. He took a greater chance this time but he believed the method he used along with the fact that he had sufficient control over his two friends would prevent them from reporting the homicides to the police. He was bothered some by the similarity of this event to his killing the wounded enemy during the war. Still, it didn't bother him enough that he would stop the homicides. He reasoned that killing was what took place in a war and as long as there were problems between his club and other biker clubs it was justified.

He had one primary rule which would determine what targets he would accept on contract and which he wouldn't accept. The target had to be an enemy to the club. His Samurai beliefs would not allow him to take the life of an innocent person, especially a child.

That would be his downfall.

EIGHTEEN

The Boy, Part 2

At a later date, the club was having difficulty with a person we'll call Fadakis, who was causing problems for the club. Fadakis was a leader of a drug organization that was encroaching into the territory Danny's group was operating in. Danny and the leaders of his bike club attempted to work through the issues with the other organization but they wouldn't budge. Just how long the problems had been going on or whether they were recent or from the past was not told to me. There were times, in order to avoid suspicion, his club would take action against another club or person two years after the altercation had taken place.

Following a discussion among the club leadership, Danny said he would eliminate Fadakis. The club leadership again pleaded with him to let someone else do the job but once Danny had made the decision to do it himself, it was impossible to change his mind.

Again, during the conversation, he experienced the emotional changes that he had experienced during discussions of prior hits. He got excited when they spoke of the need to eliminate this person and he started imagining how it would all go down as they were talking about it. As he put himself in the role of the killer, he felt excitement and then peace. He felt confident in his belief that no one could carry it off as well as he could and, by the time they completed the conversation, he had already killed Fadakis in his mind.

℃

The usual preparations were made. Danny went to where Fadakis lived in an apartment in the heart of the city. He watched Fadakis's movements for three days and planned the hit for about 2:00 AM when he knew Fadakis and his body-guard would be returning from a party. Danny did his usual routine during the day since it had become a ritual. When it came time for him to leave the motel, Danny rode his cycle into town, parked it close to where the hit would take place, and waited. He was dressed as a street person and walked as if he had been drinking. His success depended on his believ-ability.

When he saw Fadakis's Mercedes drive up to his apart-ment and stop, Danny turned the corner of the street and walked toward the car, making sure that he looked drunk. As he approached the car, Fadakis was opening the door and stepping out.

Danny had been looking down towards the ground while walking, as if he wasn't aware of the car or of the man getting out of it. When he got close to Fadakis he looked up as if surprised. He had been holding a broken cigarette in his hand as he walked that was not lit. It likely appeared to Fadakis that this street person had found a cigarette on the ground. Danny knew that if he reached into his old coat to pull out a cigarette while Fadakis was watching, it might alert Fadakis that something might be amiss.

Danny timed it so he would reach Fadakis before Fadakis closed his door. Danny walked to Fadakis and asked if he could get a light for his cigarette. As Fadakis reached for his cigarette lighter, Danny quickly pulled out his pistol and shot Fadakis.

At this point it was all over. The hit had taken place, the streets still had no cars coming towards them, and all Danny had to do was to walk back to his cycle, throw away the weapon and his gloves, drive to the safe house, and return to the club in a day or two. If someone had seen him they would likely not have been able to identify him since he looked no different than the other street people in the area.

As he turned to walk back to his cycle he caught a movement in his peripheral vision. He turned and saw a figure running across the sidewalk and down an alleyway. It didn't matter that he had been seen, but for some reason he wanted to check it out. He ran to the alley and looked. There was a streetlight at the other end enabling Danny to detect any movement in the alley. There was none.

Garbage cans were lined up behind the rear entrances of apartments and store back doors. Danny knew that someone had seen him shoot the guy and this person was likely hiding behind one of the garbage cans. Danny was on automatic and he didn't stop to consider his situation. He knew the image he saw was small so it likely wasn't an adult. It wasn't an animal. It had to be a child. But what was a child doing out on the streets at two o'clock in the morning? Still, it didn't matter. If he had been able to pause for a moment and think about what to do, he would have realized that it was only a child, and he would have gotten on his cycle and left the area. Danny was about to commit an act which would violate the single most important principle of his Samurai code.

Danny began walking down the alley, moving each trash can and looking into each back entrance. About halfway down he pulled a trash can away from a rear entrance into a building and saw a young boy crouching in the corner. The boy pleaded, "Please mister, don't kill me!" Danny shot twice. The boy was dead.

It was at this point that Danny became aware that he had just killed a boy of about twelve years of age. This was the single most traumatic event that had ever occurred in his lifetime. The loss of Philippe was hard to get over, but the death of the boy would be much harder. Danny rode his cycle to the safe house and, following his usual routine, didn't tell them what he had done.

Danny talked about the boy several times during our discussions, and each time he looked down as he spoke; he had difficulty finding the words he wanted to use and it was clear that he was re-living the act each time he talked about it. He could still hear the boy's voice pleading for his life now, several years after it had occurred.

The one last instance [killing the boy] was like it broke up everything and I couldn't put that in any spot or cover it up. The boy wasn't responsible so I couldn't put him there. I don't know why I even did it.

What do you mean you couldn't put him there? Put him where?

Out of all the people that I killed I knew why I did it to all of the others. I couldn't justify why that boy had to die. He was innocent.

Do you have full memory of having done it? I remember you talking about the group in Nam and it was like you could remember one or two of the six but you couldn't remember the others. Do you have full memory with the boy?

Yes, and I used to think that was because of the boy himself. I killed two people that night and I don't remember much about the other one. I have a picture of how it happened with the other one and I can close my eyes and see everyone I have killed if I want to take the time and find each and every one of them. I can pull each of them up as a visual. You know, like on a TV screen. I can pull the boy up too, but I can't really pull up the two that I was there to do in the first place that night.

What about dreams associated with the boy or the others?

I have had them about the boy and it has really been strange because in my dreams it never changes. It will always be in the same situation where I caused the death. Not wanting to but it is always an accident on my part that I am trying to stop.

You said before that at times you have felt somewhat haunted by the spirits and they stayed around you?

> That is exactly what I felt. I used to speak of them like they existed, and they still do exist for me and always will. It is hard to imagine that somebody would want to bring another personality into them. I think that, no matter what, that is what happens when you kill someone.

The person's spirit comes inside of you?

> I think so. I can't speak for everybody so I am just speaking for me. They become a dominant part whether you like it or not. It was like I couldn't forget and I was bothered a little bit before the boy, but I was bothered tremendously afterwards and it seems like all of a sudden there was a problem with everyone that I killed.

What do you mean?

> There were times that I felt that maybe I should not have killed the prisoners in Vietnam. Everything else was okay and all of the people I killed up until the boy was okay too. They were part of what was going on with me and they brought it upon themselves. I killed them, but they brought their death upon themselves.
>
> With the boy, I tried to somehow rationalize or put it in some sort of perspective and quickly realized that I couldn't do that so I tried to forget, and when I tried to forget I remembered everybody I had killed and I started to

question whether or not I should have done any of this. It was difficult for me to deal with and I couldn't deal with it and I have never been able to deal with it. I have been obsessed with it ever since it happened.

I was fighting the questions, I was terrified of the questions and their spirits is what was making me come back to these questions. It wasn't something that I wanted to do. I had a pretty strong will even then. If I was going to do something then I would do it. I was doing tremendous amounts of drugs that I should have been able to get away from them, but it didn't work. It didn't matter, my moods were amazing. I could be laughing one minute and just like that I would be absolutely morbid the next minute and really depressed.

Were your friends aware of your mood swings?

I would be feeling bad but acting good and that I was okay. Then what would happen is that I would get to the point where I couldn't act anymore and the pressure was so much I couldn't deal with it.

Do you have any idea of what thoughts or images would come into your mind?

It would be the whys, the reasons why. Was this wrong? And if so, what are you going to do? It got to be a question of how. If the truth was that I shouldn't have done these things, then how was I going to handle that?

. . .

What do you mean by handle that?

> How was I going to handle it mentally? I was afraid and didn't want to handle that question that this might not have been the thing to do.

Was there ever some idea that you might have to meet your maker and explain it?

> No, I have never believed in that at all and still don't believe that there is a maker who cares about whether or not this happened. What I have to be concerned with are the things that I have done and what I have to do now. My concern with me is not because of a maker, but because I believe we have honor and integrity as human beings. I violated mine, not theirs. I killed them but that was secondary to what happened to them. I killed them and stopped their existence here, but I didn't hurt their existence in their future at all. Maybe I saved them from doing something to dishonor themselves and therefore lower their position later on in another existence.
>
> I lowered my own by doing what I did and I was worried if I wasn't right and this was all wrong. I never looked at it, up until the boy, I looked at it like we were all sort of soldiers in this same thing and these guys were bad and had to be taken care of. I didn't feel like they had to die, but if they did, so what? Even though knowing they were going to and I was going to die it was like so what?
>
> After the boy I couldn't say that. I had to look at the boy as much as I didn't want to look at him. Looking at the

boy opened up everything else. If you were absolutely beyond a shadow of a doubt wrong in this case is this other thing right? Those questions terrified me. I knew what was I going to do now to make this right and I couldn't see any other way out.

NINETEEN

Haunted by Ghosts

Danny got on his cycle and left the area. He followed his usual routine of getting rid of the gun and the gloves and he drove to the safe house. The next morning the story appeared in the news about the three deaths. Danny, who generally didn't have any difficulty telling the truth, denied having killed the kid and got angry if anyone asked him about it.

You know, I had this feeling … I thought … I felt that was going to happen, you know. I felt that sooner or later a kid was going to be involved or something or something was going to happen. I had … I had those feelings. For some reason or other I had them.

At first … I refused to … admit that … I had anything to do with that. I mean … I didn't come up with a good lie. I didn't come up with any lie is the thing. I just said I didn't do it. They said, "Okay, okay. You didn't do that." They didn't make up a lie like, "Well, somebody must have come along and picked up the gun and.…"

. . .

When you shot the boy, was there anything in your mind that tried to stop you?

> Yeah, there was. I can remember like … it was like a … he was talking but it was … a screaming "No!" in my head, like it was … like … I don't even know why. I don't even know why. I don't know why that I even went after him. It just don't make no sense. It never did, it never did from the moment afterwards, it never made any sense to me. I knew that I was through, that I was going to pay for this.

When he got back to the club headquarters he was still haunted by what he had done. His life began to change.

> In about a month, I lost interest in everything I was involved with at the time, everything with the club. Everything else. I said I needed time. I needed a vacation. I needed to be away from things. I'd been working too hard. You know, like some person that's got a job and he's working too much. And I was allowed to go to hell actually is what happened.

His friends respected him and they gave him his space hoping he would snap out of it. If they were disturbed by what he did, they didn't say so. They may have been bothered by what happened to the boy, but they were bothered even more by the changes they saw in Danny.

It was very difficult for Danny to talk about killing the boy. His voice became softer, he hesitated when he spoke and he had difficulty finding the words he wanted to use. He couldn't understand why he had killed the boy because it was his policy to protect the innocent.

I did do that. I looked out for people, the weaker people. I'm talking about women and children and stuff. And old men and things. I did do that. That's what made it altogether wrong and I ... I could never get ... I could never make it right in my head. I couldn't ... I knew from that moment on that was it. And you know what? I denied the whole damn thing all the way down the line. Everybody remotely involved with this knew I did that [killing the boy]. Everybody denied it too. I denied it. Everybody else denied it. You could look at me and tell I did it but I did not admit it. I wouldn't admit it.

Was it after this that you began thinking about other people you had killed?

It wasn't like right away. It was like all I could think about was the kid for a long time. I didn't have to kill him and I couldn't understand why I did. I'd wake up thinking about him and I'd crash thinking about him. We could be having this conversation and I'd be thinking about him, just like I'm thinking about him now. You know, it's like once I start thinking about him, still to today, it's hard for me to get it away.

How real is the image in your mind?

It's extremely real right now.

Real enough that you can close your eyes and almost feel yourself there again?
Yeah.

As if it's imprinted on your mind?

You know something? I've tried to … I don't know why … I don't know if everybody does this, but I've tried to change the memories a thousand times. A million times. I've tried to change … change it, stop it, change it. I've never been able to. I don't know. I think this is the core of everything for me. It's like no matter what I do, no matter what I try … I can't dodge this bullet. You know?

You know what it was? I think I was living this lie … that I still felt … that I was honorable, that what I was doing had some validity on some level or another but that even if I was right … there was no way after the boy … I've thought about it so much that … I couldn't ever really justify it … get that together.

In what ways did this change you?

I drank a lot, not that I didn't before, but I did more. I never took a breath that I wasn't stoned and … drunk and high. I would do dope and I was really violent. I got really violent all the time. Like I would punch my friends. As soon as I got up in the morning I would start getting high. Alcohol really helped, I have to admit. Drugs and alcohol really helped me through that time. I know it sounds crazy but ... I used those things completely different to try to get something in my life.

Danny was pulling away from his friends and from his responsibilities in the club. He wasn't able to talk to even his closest friends about killing the boy, and by denying it he wasn't able to tell them how badly he felt about what he had done. Guilt plagued him and much of his time was taken up attempting to find ways to avoid thinking about the boy. He became confused about the meaning of the life he had been living.

It was like I had no feeling at all for anything. It was like nothing made any sense. I mean nothing. Even the stuff I had been doing that usually made sense. Life didn't make any sense. Nothing mattered. Nothing mattered to me. It was directly because of what had happened, but I wasn't willing to recognize that. I wasn't owning up to it.

The guilt was overpowering. He couldn't sleep it off, he couldn't drink it away, and drugs didn't allow him to avoid the memories. However, like many people do, a combination of drugs and alcohol along with an attempt to remain busy helped temporarily.

I had probably done the best job in my life that I had ever been able to do in putting something completely out of my mind and not dealing with it at all, but it was not out of my subconscious. Any time that I would get even remotely close to this issue, in any way, shape, or form, I would do anything to stop that memory. And I was successful. I was successful at it. And I moved at really a mad pace. At least that was the appearance but I was being driven by this thing. I was doing everything … it was crazy stuff, like I would drink until I passed out. I was passing out like at 1:00 pm in the afternoon. I'd passed out before but usually it was late at night, it wasn't before lunch. I started doing drugs that I didn't do before like Demerol and Valium and stuff. I started eating them. I would just do anything. Before I was selective in the drugs I did and how much I drank and what I drank but now I wasn't discretionary at all.

His friends were very concerned about how he had changed but they were powerless to do anything about it.

I just didn't care. I did some things and I didn't care, and later on when I was told about it I would think to myself, how could I have done that? Everybody thought it was funny because it was out of character in a sense. I remember we were at this bar one night. I fell on these people's table and knocked everything on the floor and I turned around and said, "Excuse me." I usually wasn't that kind of a guy. If I knocked somebody's drink off I would have bought them another one. Now, I would throw up on the floor anywhere. Nothing seemed to matter.

. . .

His most frequent emotions were fear, guilt, and anger. When he was in Vietnam he lost the ability to have peace, and ever since he had been unable to experience the subtle nuances of feelings that contribute to lasting happiness. In an attempt to grapple with his self-doubt and confusion he began going off on his own to try to think it over. His friends attempted to support him but it didn't work.

I'm talking about people didn't matter. It seemed like everything was so dull anyway. Even though they tried to be really intense with me, saying something to me like how much they loved me and this and that and stuff, it had absolutely no affect.

The intensity and the effect of their caring was small compared to the intensity of his overpowering guilt. However, Danny had always had a strong personality and it was paramount to him that he maintain control of himself. It was his friends that caused him to realize what he was doing to himself. They began to criticize his behavior.

Actually, I was doing so much dope it was really out of hand. That went on for a while and everybody and their brother was bitching at me. Not really bitching at me but everybody was worried. I couldn't get a moment's peace. Wherever I would go the conversation would eventually get around to them telling me that I was going to kill myself if I didn't stop. And I just quit. I stopped doing everything

except for heroin. This was about two months after...
after....

Why did you stop all the drugs except the heroin?

There's a lot of things that I can take but one thing I never
could take is not knowing what I did, you know? Everybody I ran into was telling me stuff that I had no idea I had
done. My whole world was starting to not make any sense
because of it.

I didn't know why people were reacting the way they
were. The woman I was with at the time was freaking out.
She was dying. She wouldn't eat because of what I was
going through. She just stopped eating, stopped everything.
She got real nervous. She lost a whole lot of weight. People
that really cared about me and cared about her said I would
be a lot kinder if I just shot her in the head or something.
Quit killing her in degrees like that. I started thinking
about that and I really started noticing. It took a while.
Like I said, I never quit heroin. I kept doing heroin. I
started realizing a lot of things.

So, you quit all of the drugs you were taking except the heroin? Did the heroin work by itself?

No, the heroin alone would not keep the memories away.
Once I stopped all these other drugs it was even harder to
keep them away.

What kind of memories? Just of the kid or other things?

Well, predominately the kid but the whole thing. That's when I first started picking up the ghosts. They started staying with me. It got to where I knew that every time I was alone I had about two minutes and then the place was going to be full of these people. You know what I'm talking about? It sounds really weird, and it is really weird but it was like I started seeing everybody I had ever killed.

Ghosts?

Yeah. The ghosts of the people I had killed.

Were these ghosts of the people you killed when you were in the bike club or were they also ghosts of people you killed when you were in Vietnam?

Both. Those at home and the prisoners I killed in Nam.

When you saw them, were they outside of you or in your head?

In my head but they were so real in my head it was like they were in the room.

What would they be doing as you were seeing them?

> Actually, they would be accusing me. I guess I felt like that was my subconscious telling me that I should have remorse for this or something or other. I don't exactly know what it was telling me but they were ... they never actually said anything. They never talked to me but I heard them in a ... but it was just the ... the ... the look of them. The feeling from them. It was accusatory. They were accusing me.

What effect did this have on you?

> I went through a long period where I was constantly arguing with myself over the right and the wrong of the situation. It was like a dog chasing its tail. It would go on until I would be exhausted, absolutely be exhausted from it running around my head. Like it ... I was just through, completely blown, because I'd keep chasing this thing in my head trying to find the answer that would give me peace. I couldn't ever find peace, though. I would give up and then the whole process would start later. I'd get a respite and then the whole process would start again and it would speed up and up and up until I reached the same point. Then I'd give up, not because I wanted to give up but because my head would just quit.

What do you mean?

> It was like I'd just keep thinking. I'd have this thought then I'd have another thought, like contradictory, and then I'd

have this other thought and this justification, then I'd go back to the first thought and this justification. Like a dog chasing its tail. It was the same thing.

And it would speed up.

Yeah, until it would get to a point where I'd be exhausted. There was no answer. It would start over again. It got to a point where it was really, really crazy, then it would stop. Then it would come back, maybe not right away. Maybe I'd be cool for a little while, a couple of days or something, and then it would come back. Eventually it would come back.

He could be in a conversation with somebody and a word or a thought would trigger the memory of the boy. Then memories of others he had killed would come into his mind. He said, "I could be having a conversation, sitting around having a conversation with you, and have the images in my head at the same time."

Like you were being haunted.

All the time. Constantly! Even when I met you and Kate down here I was haunted all the time then. It was the same thing. I had been going through that a long time.

Is it happening right now?

As we speak? Yeah, but it's not at the intensity that it used to be. I still don't have an answer. You know what I mean? I still don't have an answer. I know the facts, but there's still not the feeling about why I did it. I know on an intellectual level why I shot that boy but I don't feel it in my heart. If I felt it in my heart I could probably say, "Well, hell, I'm not that bad of a guy. I'm okay."

What is your belief about the spirits of people you killed?

Every time you kill someone you lose part of you but you gain part of them. When a person goes across to the other side [dies] something goes and something stays. The part that stays with me because I caused them to go across. This provides an eternal link with them. We are linked together forever. I sometimes feel very old, as though I've lived a number of times.

I was changed by every one of the people I killed but it was not due to grief or remorse. They all become part of me. All of them come into me. The ability to love and to be cruel partly come from them if it was their personality characteristics. When I fell in love with this girl it seemed it wasn't me, but him, one of my victims. I was a little different after I killed each one. People could tell there was something different in me and they would ask what was wrong.

Danny was unable to adjust to the death of the boy but his anger was still triggered by people who threatened his club, and at such time he would engage in a short fantasy of how he could kill them. He commented about this,

I'm not going to sit here and tell you I couldn't kill somebody. That's crazy. I can still kill somebody and I'm aware of that, but it would have to be out of anger. There's no way … after the kid, there's no way that I could kill as easily as I did. Before the kid I felt like I was defending myself. Defending us, making sure nobody hurt us and, if somebody tried, they were through.

There's been a lot of other things that I've been involved with as well. There were a lot of beatings, a lot of people hurt really bad. It's not just the killing but I feel guilty about those other things I participated in as well as the killing.

At my father's funeral he was dead and I knew I would see him in 70 years or so. When I caused a death I never thought for a minute that I wouldn't see these people either. I didn't care if I saw them. I would kill them again if I ran into them in another existence, if that was possible. I felt they should have been killed this time and I'd feel the same in the next life if I saw them again, so what's the difference?

It was as if you were back in the war?

Yeah, to me it was war. You know what I mean? But after the kid I began to realize that I gave myself all those weak excuses about that. The excuses weren't for real. I knew they weren't for real. They were weak excuses but I could make them real. I could make them work.

TWENTY

Broken Samurai

After a few months Danny left the club. In an effort to explain why, he used the example of a young girl who was close to her father but then he molested her. He said that even if her father had only molested her a couple of times and then never did it again, she may still love him because he was her father and because in some ways they had a good relationship. Still, there would always be something between them that would never be fully resolved.

Danny felt he had let his friends down and he had violated their trust. They cared deeply for him and they didn't want him to leave.

Did you go into a depression?

> Yeah, I was depressed. Actually, if you want to really look at it I probably was always depressed up to the time I walked into this room about a year ago and started talking about it. It was just that drugs were my escape. When I was not loaded everything was a struggle, always a struggle. I had to

always project something that I wasn't. That's why I had to leave. That's why I had to leave them because I couldn't … I just could not do this anymore.

What do you mean by projecting something that you weren't?

I was living a lie. My friends and the other members of the club had looked up to me as a leader. I couldn't look them in the eye and tell them to follow my example.

Did your Samurai beliefs have anything to do with you leaving?

Definitely. As I said before, even as a small child I was fascinated with the concepts of purity, honor, and justice. With the Samurai you decide what you feel is right and wrong and you stick by it. I made the decision of what was right for me but I didn't stick by it. To break your code is the worst thing you can possible do.

The highest concept from the Samurai is duty. Duty and honor are the same thing for a Samurai. What you have to do, you do. You know what I mean? The brothers of mine in the bike club were worthy. I had been worthy but I broke the code and I am no longer worthy. My soul is in jeopardy.

How did you get away from the club?

I took the first thing that popped up, that came along, concerning my old lady. I made a big issue out it. I told her and them, "You don't tell me what to do." They were thinking of my welfare, actually, "Never tell me what to do!" I just shunned them and it wasn't long after that that I broke it off. I took off.

Danny began going around the country. At times he was on his cycle and at times in a car. He had a number of friends throughout the country and he would visit them.

Well, I went a lot of places actually. I became a notorious outlaw after that.

Did you go into a destructive phase?

In retrospect I can look at it and … I didn't even know it at the time. That what's so crazy. But this crap I was doing, gees, there just wasn't anything that I would not do. I wasn't trying to hurt anybody, but I was robbing anything that wasn't moving. If it would hold still for a second I was going to rob it. I'd probably even have robbed a train if I'd known there was some money on it. I was gambling. I was in places I should not have been, and I was able to get out alive.

He took chances that he would never have taken before. He had dropped out of the club but the opportunity was always there for him to return. I asked him if he wanted to get caught.

I don't think I wanted to get caught. I think I wanted to get killed. I wanted to, then I didn't want to, then I wanted to. It went back and forth like that. My thought was to let the chips fall where they fall. I was going to do anything that crossed my mind.

I've been in places in cities where the other guys in my club won't go. I think they looked at me in those situations and said, "This guy's no mark. This guy's a maniac." I had guns hanging all over me everywhere. I was not just going to humbly march off and die. I was going to go down blazing with both hands. That's the way I always envisioned me dying anyway, shooting it out somehow, some way with the police or somebody. The old Jesse James syndrome, I suppose. Shooting with both hands. Always with both hands. Isn't that funny? I don't shoot but with one hand, but in my fantasies, it's always two.

I've learned something about fantasy through all of this.

Fantasy?

If a person has a fantasy about wanting to wipe out a lot of people, if he doesn't stop the fantasy it will get to the point he will carry it out. I honestly believe that because with me it was a stronger and stronger and stronger thing. At times I could be just anywhere and I'd feel like I just wanted to whip it out and phom, phom, phom, just start gunning people down. It was the dumbest thing.

Would you feel angry when you thought this way?

Yeah, I did. And you know what? It would be just a powerful feeling that even when I didn't do it I'd feel like … afterwards, I'd feel … calm.

That's very interesting. You're saying that a fantasy of engaging in violence against people would calm you down rather than get you all excited about actually carrying it out. Why would the fantasy of violence calm you down?

Because I began to feel I could do it. I could actually do it. At first, when I would think about going in and shooting up a place I would think, "Nah, I can't do that. I can't do that." But the more you think about it, the more you start thinking, "Yeah, I can do that." You smile secretly to yourself like, "Uh huh, I just did you all in and I can. If I want to, I can." This is the point where it becomes really dangerous because along there somewhere you go ahead and do it.

Let's talk about more about that. You're saying that if a person is angry and they want to kill a lot of people they may initially hold back because part of them is saying that they can't do it? Or shouldn't do it?

I'll tell you, that even scared me. I even felt like this is getting out of hand. I don't know how I snapped to it but one day I snapped to that and I'm thinking in terms of that I can do this, and it was almost like I had already done it.

But you hadn't done it. It seems logical that when your thoughts changed from thinking you couldn't do it to thinking you could do it you would become more energized about the possibility of carrying it out. Talk about the connection between the thought that you could actually go ahead and do it and the thought causing you to feel calm.

When I'd get the feeling that I wanted to kill a bunch of people it was when I was angry and depressed. But when I thought of it, I felt anxious. I'd fantasize pulling out my pistol and pow, pow, pow, shooting them and seeing everybody running and screaming and everything.

But you wouldn't do it.

No, but the fantasy would be real and I would feel like it had already been done and I'd feel really good about it. I'd feel calm.

Again, what would cause the calm feeling? Would it be a peaceful feeling?

A big negative feeling about shooting a bunch of people down is that you are going to get blown away yourself. That was the thing I always thought about in those terms, like they are going to gun me down or I'm going to get wounded and the cops are going to get hold of me. After a while I started thinking ... I remember too, I remember exactly how it went down too. I remember smiling to myself afterwards thinking that I could actually do it to all these people and there's nothing they can do about it. There was nothing that nobody could do about it.

But you already knew that there was nothing anybody could do about it. If you went into a place and began blasting away, nobody could stop you at first. If there was a cop there and he shot you, it could stop it. However, you knew all of that. Was it the feeling of power?

Absolutely. And I think that in the end that's what kicks most people over the edge. They get the feeling that they can and then they are gone. If you don't immediately grab that and say, "Wait a minute. What is this?" and look at it intellectually, like, "What the hell is this? This cannot be. I cannot do this."

It's a progression thing. If you keep on thinking about revenge it just keeps going until you do it. When he begins thinking that he wants to do it, it may go on for years even, but there comes a point where he thinks, "Yeah, I can do this and there's nothing they can do." At that point it's not in terms of getting caught. It's in terms of these people not being able to stop you. They're all through and that feeling overrides any thought of the possibility of getting caught or killed. Once you determine that you can do it, you're less concerned that you are going to get caught or get shot. You're thinking that if you do it all of these people are through, and that overrides the fear of doing it. Then you really are dangerous.

How would you pull off the robberies? Would you plan them?

Absolutely not. I would see a place and I would rob it in about five minutes. Sometimes I would drive half the night across Illinois and I'd see some place in a town and I'd say, "This place." Then I'd go in and rob it. It didn't matter, it really didn't matter.

Would you not care if anybody walked in?

I was robbing the place and I didn't want any more hassles than I had to get out of it, but I did some strange things. Like I robbed a drive-through in a store. I robbed a lot of those. Somebody could drive through at any moment. There was not that much money. You're talking $500 or $600 to $1,000.

Would you be in a car or on your cycle?

Usually I'd be in a car. I remember walking up to this place one night. It was a drive-through. At first I looked through the window and I saw this guy and he picked up a broom and he walked towards the drive-through area. I stepped inside the building and pulled the ski mask down over my face and I pulled my pistol out and I was holding it like this [he demonstrates]. Over on this other side there was a door. There were three aisles there that had chips and stuff. I was standing here and with this pistol in my hand and here comes a kid about eight years old. He jerked the door open and came through. He was running and so it was right there in front of me in just a couple of seconds. Like I'm standing there waiting for this guy to step back [the sweeper to step back from the drive-through window] inside. This kid runs in and stops right there in front of me. I look at the kid and he looks at me. He stands there looking at me and he turns around and runs out again. I figured somebody drove up and stopped and let the kid come in to get something. So, I turn around and go out the door I came in and go over this little hill. I suppose the kid ran out and told his parents there was a guy in there with a gun and a mask on. They probably called the police. Nobody saw me but this little boy, and I figured everybody probably thought the boy had lied.

At times Danny wore a ski mask and other times he wouldn't. On one occasion he robbed a store that was a few blocks from a police station. He did most of his robberies by himself but there were times when he had a friend with him.

I was thinking all the time about my death, trying to envision how it would be. I had these fantasies about going into the police station and shooting it out with the cops. Always the cops. For some reason I felt they had something to do with something. Actually, they were only doing their job. I understand that now but … at the time they were some sort of an enemy I could focus on.

Did you have nightmares?

When I cut back on the dope I had them but usually they were day-mares. Like I'd nod off or something during the day, or it would be during a stretch when I wasn't heroined out. If I was heroined out, I wouldn't have any nightmares. And I'd do heroine morning and night.

How complete were these flashbacks or day-mares?

Not very because I wouldn't allow them to stay. You know? I'd do whatever I had to do, whatever. Whatever it took to get rid of it.

What images or thoughts would primarily come into your mind?

It was funny because anything could trigger anything. Like I could be seeing a movie or I could be reading a book or I could see kids or I could see a girlfriend. Everything was so tied in, you see, because I hardly ever thought about one thing. I always thought about all of these things. Once it started everything got covered until the point of exhaustion and then it would stop. I don't care where you started it at, it runs all the way through. You could start it here in the middle and then catch the end and then catch the beginning and back through and around and around and through it all.

The same sequence of events? The same sequence of memories?

Not the same sequence but the same memories. It would be different sequences but the same bunch would be covered every time.

These hauntings didn't stop. Danny kept pulling off robberies throughout the state, hoping he would be killed. The police finally caught up with him when he robbed a store and then robbed a bank. He was found guilty and was sentenced to do time in the state prison for the store robbery and, following his release, he would be transferred to a federal prison to do his time there for the bank robbery. His arrests were for robbery only since there was no evidence to prove that he had committed a homicide. While in the state prison he got into a therapy program. He was against changing because he thought he hadn't done anything that was exceptionally wrong. He gradually began to understand how it all had happened and he accepted responsibility for it.

The only task that remained in this research project was to clarify what he planned to do about his future. He had violated the Samurai code as he interpreted it. Could he find a way to atone for what he had done and find peace in his life?

TWENTY-ONE

Ritual Suicide

The time came to bring an end to our sessions. Danny had been exceptionally open about his life; it's rare that a veteran will reveal himself to the degree that Danny did. Other than what he personally gained from our discussions, he was given no benefits from participating in my study. That is, it didn't help him get out of prison any sooner and he obtained no special privileges while he was in prison.

Danny was obsessed with his death. It wasn't about when he would die but how it would happen. He didn't plan on a natural death. He didn't want to die of old age and he didn't want to die from medical or health problems. His interpretation of the Samurai Code allowed him to select and fight an enemy after he returned home from the war but it also ascribed to him the manner in which he must die if he were to violate the code.

I know what I will have to do now to make this right. I can't see any other choice. I have to restore my honor and integrity.

. . .

What do you mean?

> It has to be done the way the Samurai did it. It has to take will power. It has to be a ritual, a purification ritual.

Where did that idea come from?

> As I said before, I have always been fascinated by the code of honor that the Samurai had. Somehow, I have always understood what they were doing. They were harsh and cruel. They were cold. But they were also absolutely honorable. What they did was perfect justice. They had perfect knowledge of what it was all about. What they did to others had to be okay if they turned around and did it to themselves in that regard.

What are you referring to?

> The boy.

Danny's voice changed. It became soft, he strung out his words, he looked down. He struggled to get through this next part.

I think this right here is the core for everything for me. It's like no matter what I do, no matter what I try I ... can't dodge this bullet. You know? It's at the bottom of me. I ... have to pay for that one.

What has to happen?

I have my own belief of what has to be. I ... if ... if ... blood atonement is the only thing.

What do you think will happen, or will have to happen for you to pay for this?

I'm ... I'm ... I'm after my soul. I believe if you do certain things in life you may ... you do irreversible damage to your soul. I'm not ... just killing isn't enough. Killing is not wrong. It's who you kill and how you kill and why you kill ... certain things you have to ... you have to ... somehow pay it back. I can't do anything other than somehow restore my honor to me.

When I talk about honor, my soul is an honorable thing. If I don't set it right, if I don't set this thing right ... I don't believe this is the end of anything. When we die, it's not the end of nothing. Actually, maybe having that belief, cause I've had it forever, is another reason why killing wasn't such a terrible thing. Except as regards to the kid. For some reason that is terrible.

It's like I have to prove my courage. I have to wash my soul. I have to pay the price, life for life. Not that ... not that it means ... not that this is the end of anything. I'm just saying that the next life I have, or the next existence I have if I don't want it to be terrible ... if I don't want it to be terrible this has ... this has to be done to set things right.

How might you do that?

I have my own ... it's ritual suicide done in a certain way to claim the most from the ritual. There's a method of ... the same thing a lot of the Samurai used. Not a lot because most of them didn't do it that way. In truth, it's a method of where you take a knife and you put it under your rib and you take it all the way down to your groin. You make four strokes, from the top to your belly, then down to your groin. Then you insert the knife in your side and go to the middle and from there to the other side. Then you ... you have to pull your intestines out yourself. You've got to do it all without any noise. You can't utter any cries. You ... die that way.

As he was telling me this, there was no doubt in my mind he was sincere. Although he didn't believe in God or in heaven, he believed that he would see his father again in the next existence. Undoubtedly he believed that his father had passed the tests he was required to go through in this life and would be moving to a happier and a more peaceful plane in the next life. Danny wanted to be with him.

He believed that Philippe had also gone to his reward, as had other friends of his who died in the Vietnam War. The thousands of soldiers who gave their lives for our country during the war would also be rewarded for their sacrifice even though they had no understanding of the principles of Samurai. They had fulfilled their duty and they were honorable.

Danny saw his situation as different from his father's, Phillippe's, or the others. They died innocently. Danny, however, believed that because of his understanding of the principles of the Samurai he would be held to a higher level of accountability for his actions. Killing was not wrong as he saw it, it was who you killed and how you killed. The boy was innocent and Danny would have to pay for killing him in the next life. Danny was no longer worthy of an exalted place as an honorable warrior. This could mean that Danny may not get to be with his father or Philippe. And, when he was reincarnated back into another life, he would have to suffer in order to atone for the boy. There's no greater hell a reincarnated Samurai warrior can go through than to be a disgrace to his code.

Only a purification ritual would suffice to atone for the boy.

However, Danny died before he had the chance to rescue himself from his self-made hell.

Epilogue

Danny is dead.

We can say that it's all Danny's fault, that if he had not gotten involved with drugs and criminal activities after the war he could have lived an honorable life as a respected member of society. It's said that every person carves out his own destiny from the potter's clay given him. Did Danny choose to become violent? Was he a psychopath who felt no guilt over destroying people? If so, why did he feel a need to protect innocent people like women, children, and old men?

Danny's technique for surviving was to be an aggressor. He had identified with the Samurai and the Samurai Code since he was in middle school. He wanted to be tough, skilled as a fighter, a defender of the poor, and a fighter against injustice. To him, the war was good guys pitted against bad guys and he wanted to be a leader among the good guys. As an aggressor, he believed he increased his chances to survive, or to possibly be killed. He didn't care which. He had studied Bushido and he believed he was a reincarnated Samurai Warrior and, being such, whatever he did in the realm of good against evil that was within the boundaries of the Code. As he saw it, was justified. If he did get killed in the war he would die honorably and his reward in the next life would be great. To die was not the end of anything. Duty and loyalty were everything.

There can be no question that Danny had PTSD. Did his PTSD have anything to do with him becoming a hit man? Why couldn't he find a way of dealing with his traumatic memories while living a law-abiding life?

Once he was in the biker club where he had all the money, drugs, alcohol, women, and status he wanted, why did he feel a need to become a contract killer? And, finally, why couldn't he consider the killing of the boy as collateral damage? After all, even if he didn't kill a child during the war, some of his Marine friends likely did, and Danny would have comforted them by explaining it's just what happens in war. Why couldn't Danny give himself the same advice? Why did he so completely fall apart because of killing the boy?

Why did Danny kill the boy? He considered the boy to be innocent. He said he could continue destroying the enemy because it was war and he swore that he would never kill an innocent person. He knew the boy couldn't identify him. He was aware that the longer he remained near the crime scene after having killed his two victims the greater the chance that someone would drive by and see what had happened. He knew that his friends in the club would never tolerate the killing of a child and they would be ashamed of him if he did it. There was absolutely no gain from killing the boy and there were several reasons why it was totally wrong. Why then did he kill the boy?

Was it an act of self-destruction? The shots he fired into the boy's chest were not because of a desire to kill the boy. Was it to stop himself from his life of crime? He said that as Danny he would be hesitant to make a decision to harm others, but as Charlie he didn't think of anything other than engaging in the action without any qualms or questions about it. Was the part of him who was identified as Danny attempting to destroy the uncontrolled side he referred to as Charlie? Some killers I have known appeared to have set themselves up to be caught.

It's clear that Danny had to be held accountable for his behavior. He had been put in prison for robbery and was aware that his sentence would be much longer if he got caught again. Still, the threat of a long prison sentence didn't stop him from entering into a broad criminal lifestyle.

Danny only understood the path he had chosen in retrospect. At the time, he had been so numbed by the experience of war and death, particularly Phillipe's demise at the hands of the enemy, that his experience wasn't so much that he was making choices but instead simply putting one foot in front of the other. But the anger, depression, and conditioning to use violence led him to his destruction.

Danny's training in the Marines was to use violence first in dealing with the enemy. His experience in Vietnam, particularly during the three months of bombardment at Khe Sanh, reinforced beliefs that he already held, particularly that family comes first, violence is sometimes necessary to protect your family, and warriors can gain honor by fighting the good fight. Vietnam also stripped him of every emotion but anger, depression and, for brief periods, excitement. The term "trauma" doesn't begin to express the damage done to Danny's mind and body. The war stole his humanity.

My understanding of combat PTSD has increased exponentially because Danny was willing to allow me to explore the details of his life. But what of the responsibility of the government? Or the rest of us? If a person is trained to kill and is given permission to do so and then is placed in an environment where he has to do it in order to survive, can we fully blame him for not being able to revert back to his pre-war personality after the war is over? But then the majority of combat vets don't continue killing after they get home, even if they did a lot of it in the military. Granted, Danny's case is extreme, but there are many damaged veterans like Danny. For those who don't get involved in crime, many still have their lives destroyed from the experience of war. Maybe the best we can do is to offer training on how to survive the trauma of killing and living around death, rather than simply training a soldier to kill.

If the government understands how to cope with the epidemic of PTSD, they aren't using that knowledge to its best effect. I would rather speculate that they don't really know what to do about it. Offering PTSD therapy not only from the government but also from other therapists and trauma programs around the country would help. A directed effort in the civilian therapist community to help these damaged men and women could make an enormous difference. In my opinion, we have the responsibility to try.

What we are doing for war veterans is not enough.

Appendix

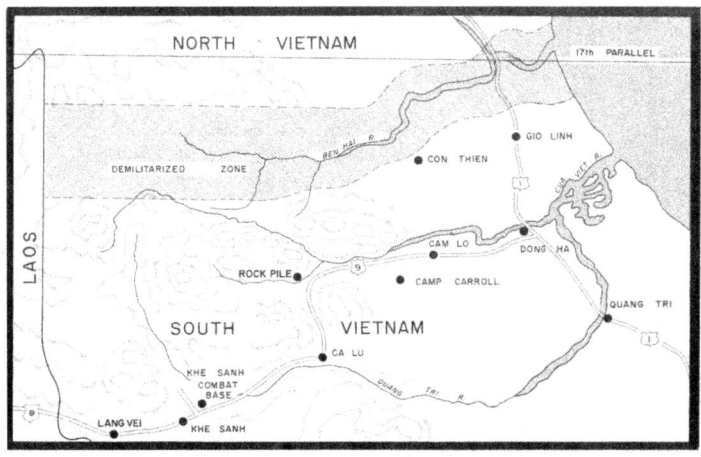

Vietnam Demilitarized Zone (DMZ)

Acknowledgments

There are many people who have helped with this book. First and foremost, appreciation needs to go to Kate, the therapist who worked with Danny before I got to know him. If she had not introduced Danny to me this project would never have started. Her therapeutic expertise allowed Danny to feel safe when I asked him to reveal the private details of his life.

Thanks also go to Dr. Michael R. Collings who reviewed the entire book and gave valuable suggestions which were incorporated into the book.

My agent Carrie Anne Keller has been an invaluable asset in encouraging me to do this project.

I greatly appreciate the late Danny for his willingness to share his story with me, and in addition, special thanks need to go to other combat veterans who also shared the details of their war experiences with me.

Since this book first was published, some people have had a difficult time reading it. Some have felt sorry for Danny. Veterans have said it stirred up too many memories of their own combat trauma. Some said they wanted to see some indication of hope for Danny, and for others who have fought for our country. In the second edition, I have attempted to offer hope rather than condemnation.

As a psychologist, before talking to veterans I was unaware of the extent of the overpowering effects of war them. Most vets do not talk about these things and they aren't detailed in mental health textbooks. Mental health professionals need a more complete understanding of war, even if we hear or read things that frighten us. I have reported what Danny said in his own words and I have made no attempt to dramatize it. What he said was from his heart.

━━

In this third edition, we added back the parts removed from the first edition. We feel that, while one or two items that were deleted may be hard for some people, they are important to help understand Danny and his motivations.

We do not believe that Danny's story shows there is no hope for veterans with PTSD. Rather, this book depicts one man's journey, and where his choices led him. Most do not become killers. We hope this book will help the rest of us understand PTSD a little better, and lead to more help for veterans around the world who fought for freedom and now suffer because of it. We also hope that, by understanding Danny, we can recognize a pattern of violence to protect kids from predators, or from becoming predators.

About the Author

The majority of Al Carlisle's career was as a psychologist at the Utah State Prison from which he retired as the head of the Psychology Department in 1989. He continued to interview serial killers. He wanted to learn why good people chose to do bad things.

Dr. Carlisle performed the first psychological assessment of Ted Bundy in 1976 while he was being held for a 90-day evaluation at the Utah State Prison.

Dr. Carlisle was also a consultant for the Salt Lake Rape Crisis Center for several years and hosted workshops on serial homicide and other crime topics. He conducted extensive research on serial killers and interviewed the Hi Fi killers, Arthur Gary Bishop, Westley Allan Dodd, Keith Jesperson, Ted Bundy and many others.

His specialties include Dissociative Identity Disorder (Multiple Personality Disorder).

Al Carlisle, born and raised in Utah, received a BS and MS from Utah State University and his Ph.D. in clinical psychology from Brigham Young University.

Dr. Carlisle passed away in 2018 at the age of 81.
https://www.alcarlisle.com

Also by Al Carlisle, PhD

Books in the *Development of the Violent Mind* series:

1: *"I'm Not Guilty!" The Case of Ted Bundy*

2: *Mind of the Devil: The Cases of Arthur Gary Bishop & Westley Allan Dodd*

3: *Broken Samurai: One Marine's Journey from Hero to Hitman*

4: *The 1976 Psychological Assessment of Ted Bundy*

5: *The Ted Bundy Files: A 1976 Companion*

Publisher's Note

The stories and recollections in this book are taken from interviews and correspondence with "Danny." The accuracy of these events may be marred with historic discrepancies due to the passage of time and the cognitive nature of PTSD.

This book has triggered a couple of people with PTSD. We had several former military read the book before publication. They said it brought back unwelcome memories, but they didn't want it changed because of its accurate depiction. While there are no graphic details, those with PTSD should be aware of this.

This book is about one man's journey, one man's choice. Very few Veterans end up like Danny, but many have a hard time adapting to life after war. Some end up living on the streets. Some go from job to job, unable to stick with anything. Others end up staying indoors, hiding from the world. There is hope and there is help.

Many factors that are not combat-related can cause PTSD. This book may trigger some, but it can also help others understand what it's like, and perhaps have more empathy for those suffering from PTSD.

There is good and evil in each one of us. To quote Professor Dumbledore, "It is our choices...that show what we truly are, far more than our abilities." The same can be said about choosing to act on thoughts and desires that we know are wrong. The people in Dr. Carlisle's books began as basically good people, but they made choices that led them step-by-step down a path to prison. We hope Dr. Carlisle's books give you a greater understanding of the development of the violent mind.

Charlene & Carrie Anne
   Two blind ladies with cats.

Quote from *Harry Potter and the Chamber of Secrets* by J. K. Rowling